"You're my mistress now, Iseult, in my bed until I say so…"

Rebellion quivered in Iseult's belly. "What about me? Don't I have any say in this?"

He shook his head, again the reality chafing. No other woman had ever questioned his intentions. "Not really, *habiba.*"

Distracted for a second, Iseult asked, "What does that mean, *habiba?*" He'd called her that a few times over the past night.

Nadim's mouth twisted for a moment. Something dark crossed his face and then with clear reluctance he said, "It means *beloved*…but it's just a figure of speech."

He put a finger under Iseult's chin, his voice hard. "I know how your first lover can inspire feelings…. Don't fall in love with me, Iseult. I *won't* be responsible for your heart."

ABBY GREEN deferred doing a social anthropology degree to work freelance as an assistant director in the film and TV industry—which is a social study in itself! Since then it's been early starts, long hours, mucky fields, ugly car parks and wet-weather gear—especially working in Ireland. She has no bona fide qualifications but could probably help negotiate a peace agreement between two warring countries after years of dealing with recalcitrant actors. She discovered a guide to writing romance one day, and decided to capitalize on her longtime love for Harlequin romances and attempt to follow in the footsteps of such authors as Kate Walker and Penny Jordan. She's enjoying the excuse to be paid to sit inside, away from the elements. She lives in Dublin and hopes that you will enjoy her stories. You can email her at abbygreen3@yahoo.co.uk.

BREAKING THE SHEIKH'S RULES

ABBY GREEN

~ KINGS OF THE DESERT ~

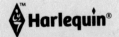
Harlequin®

TORONTO NEW YORK LONDON
AMSTERDAM PARIS SYDNEY HAMBURG
STOCKHOLM ATHENS TOKYO MILAN MADRID
PRAGUE WARSAW BUDAPEST AUCKLAND

Recycling programs
for this product may
not exist in your area.

ISBN-13: 978-0-373-88177-2

BREAKING THE SHEIKH'S RULES

First North American Publication 2011

Copyright © 2010 by Abby Green

BREAKING THE SHEIKH'S RULES

This is for Peter Commane—thank you
for answering all of my questions
and for showing me around Goffs, and for
demonstrating how to bid on a yearling
in the process; here's to Sheila's Wish!

Thanks also to Nemone
for taking the time to answer my queries.

CHAPTER ONE

SHEIKH NADIM BIN KALID AL SAQR'S dark eyes
followed the horse and rider as they exercised on
the gallops. He was blinded not only by the sheer
magnificence of the colt, which had quickened his
pulse and sent a thrill of triumph through him as
soon as he'd seen its exquisite lines, but also by
the intense green of everything as far as the eye
could see. Softly falling rain covered everything
in a fine mist, even though it was an unseasonably
warm September day.

For a man who considered himself hewn from
the uncompromising aridity of mountains and
desert, he hadn't expected to feel a kinship with
this inclement part of the world, but strangely,
standing here now, he felt its lushness pull on his
soul in a way he hadn't anticipated.

Up until now he'd been content to confine his
interest in thoroughbred racing and breeding to
his home on the Arabian peninsula, trusting his
aides to buy in Europe and transport the horses

to him. But now it was time to set up a European base, and he'd chosen Kildare, the Irish capital of thoroughbred breeding and training.

Ireland's reputation as home to the world's best horses, breeders and trainers was not in doubt. The man beside him, despite his florid appearance, which more than hinted at a drinking problem, had reputedly been one of the best trainers in the world, but until very recently had all but disappeared from the racing world.

The silence grew taut but he didn't speak for a few moments longer, unperturbed, studying the two-year-old.

His eyes drifted up from the horse to the rider. He could see that not only was the horse perhaps one of the most magnificent he'd seen in a long time, the rider too was one of the most accomplished he'd seen—and that included his own carefully handpicked staff back home. He looked to be about eighteen, slim build, definitely young. Yet he exuded an effortless way of handling the horse which Nadim knew only came from true talent, sheer courage and experience. And the animal was spirited.

The man moved restlessly beside him and Nadim took pity, saying finally, 'He's a stunning colt.'

'Yes,' Paddy O'Sullivan said with more than a hint of relief in his voice. 'I was sure you'd see it straight away.'

The horse they observed and spoke of was one of the main reasons for Nadim's visit to Ireland, and the reason why he was about to buy Paddy O'Sullivan out of his failing modest-sized training grounds and stud farm.

'It'd be hard not to see it,' Nadim murmured, his eyes once again mesmerised by the sleek move of powerful muscles under the thoroughbred's glossy coat. Already he was imagining the lineage that such a stallion and his brood mares could produce one day.

He'd sent his most senior equestrian aide to research this part of the world for him, and had instantly seen the potential; the stud was about two miles down the road from the house and training grounds. Perfect for his European base.

His mouth firmed when he recalled how his aide had been all but run off the beleaguered property by some angry woman with a rabid dog—hence his advice to steer well clear. But Nadim had made sure that his people had approached Paddy O'Sullivan directly and made an offer that no drowning man hoping for a life-raft could refuse...

The O'Sullivan stud had once been very successful, breeding numerous winners. It was that pure bloodline which had produced this colt, who was already making a name for itself, having won two of Ireland's highest-profile flat races in recent months. Excitement kicked low in Nadim's belly—a sensation he hadn't felt in a long time—making him aware of how rarely spontaneous emotion impacted on his day-to-day life. Just the way he liked it.

O'Sullivan spoke again, 'Iseult has been working with him tirelessly. He wouldn't be the horse he is today without her.'

Nadim frowned and took his eyes off the horse for a moment to look down at the much shorter man beside him. He hadn't heard that name before, and assumed it had to be of Irish origin. 'Ee—sult?'

The man gestured with his white head to the field, blue eyes fond. 'Iseult is my daughter—my eldest. She's got the gift. Been able to communicate with and control every animal she's encountered since she was barely walking.'

Nadim's eyes went back to the rider on the horse. He felt slightly stunned. That was a *girl*? And this *girl* had trained this colt? Impossible; he'd worked with plenty of female trainers, but never one so young. Too young—no matter how innate her talent might be.

He shook his head, mentally trying to take it in, and only then started to see the subtle differences. Her waist dipped in and out more than a boy's should. The silhouette of her shoulders was slight, the hint of her neck delicate. Apart from that he couldn't tell much else, because she was covered up in jeans and a fleece, hair tucked up and under a flat cap. His belly clenched as he tasted the old fear when he realised belatedly that she wasn't wearing a hard hat. He drove it down. This wasn't Merkazad. The ground was soft here—not fatally hard.

But still she should be wearing adequate protection. A surge of irritation prickled across Nadim's skin. If she was at *his* stables right now she'd be seriously reprimanded for not wearing appropriate head protection.

O'Sullivan said now, *sotto voce*, even though no one could overhear, 'I'm sorry about what happened...with your assistant. Iseult's not happy about the sale...of either our stud farm or Devil's Kiss.' He continued nervously, 'She's very attached to her home and her...' The man blustered for a moment and corrected himself, 'That is, *your* horse.'

Nadim's blood started to boil ominously. *This* girl was the person who'd practically set a dog on his assistant Adil? This was intolerable. Where Nadim came from daughters were dutiful. Independent, yes, but not openly wilful and opinionated. And they weren't trainers who looked to be barely out of their teens. He thanked his lucky stars that he'd come now. This girl, if left to her own devices, could have ruined all his chances for acquiring this property.

She was clearly bent on obstructing a sale, and right now he wouldn't put it past her to sabotage the horse he wanted so badly. He was well aware that the racing world was littered with great two-year-olds who peaked too early and never went on to achieve anything else.

Those thoughts made his voice more autocratic. 'He is about to become mine, as is your property—unless of course you've changed your mind?'

O'Sullivan blustered and stuttered, '*No*, Sheikh Nadim. I never meant that at all. It's just that Iseult has been training Devil's Kiss...so she's attached.'

Nadim flicked the man beside him a dark look, hiding the fact that he was taken aback anew to hear it confirmed that she'd trained him. And he had to admit, despite his misgivings, that the horse looked good.

'I would hope that the advantage of keeping the training grounds and stud in your name, along with being kept on as manager, is benefit enough compared to the alternative—which is that your bank is ready to throw you out on the street.'

The older man was all but wringing his hands, clearly terrified he'd offended the new landlord. 'Of course, Sheikh Nadim...I never meant to imply anything... It's just that Iseult—well, she's a bit headstrong. I hope that she doesn't offend...'

His voice trailed away as the rider slowed and came to a halt, turning the horse slowly to face where Nadim and Paddy O'Sullivan stood. Nadim watched as they approached, and the rider became more obviously a young girl. Just how old was she, anyway? he wondered as they drew closer and closer. It was impossible to tell.

He noted with increasing displeasure that she wasn't jumping off the horse to make his acquaintance.

For some reason, when his attention should have been taken by the horse, he found his eye resting curiously on its rider, his thoughts staying on her. A face was partially revealed beneath the lip of the cap. And something in his chest kicked once. Like an electric shock to his heart.

He could see that her face was exquisitely sculped—high cheekbones and a delicately firm jaw, straight nose. Her eyes were hidden by the cap, and her mouth was set in a mutinous line, but Nadim imagined that in repose it would be sensuously full. His gaze dropped and he saw the unmistakable line of slight but feminine curves beneath her T-shirt. He felt another kick then, in a more base part of his anatomy, and was astounded.

He expected such responses when he moved in sophisticated circles where mature, experienced, sensually confident women abounded. Not here in a strange country, on the edge of a green field, looking at a girl he'd moments ago dismissed as a boy. And who was irritating him more with each passing minute. Anger at his own unbidden response made the muscles in his face tighten.

Iseult O'Sullivan had hated every minute of having to exercise Devil's Kiss for the man who had come to inspect the spoils of his takeover—especially when he didn't even care enough to see what he was buying himself before he came today to sign the deal.

He'd sent an assistant to trespass on their land and take photographs, after which he'd quietly bought the adjoining land some months previously. And since then he'd been biding his time, waiting to strike—like a vulture circling over a decaying carcass—until they'd had no choice but to announce the sale. But as she looked down now, her boiling anger seemed to drain away.

She was suddenly absurdly glad to be sitting astride Devil's back, because she knew if she was standing she might not be able to remember why she was angry. Her hands gripped the reins and Devil's Kiss moved restlessly underneath her, sensing her inner agitation, his highly strung nature never too far from the surface.

The man was like something from another planet, and nothing like the stereotypical Arabic Sheikh she might have imagined if she hadn't already Googled him for information and seen pictures. And, despite having seen pictures of him, it was still hard for her to deal with the reality. He looked to be in his mid-thirties, and was as insanely good-looking as his pictures had promised. Tall, handsome, and dangerously dark.

He was wearing faded jeans which clung indecently to powerful thigh muscles, and a dark long-sleeved polo shirt, its sleeves rolled up to reveal muscled forearms. His biceps bulged against the material of his shirt, and the fine Irish mist settled over him like a glittering diamond coat. His darkly olive skin stood out against the lush backdrop like an exotic hothouse flower.

One booted foot was lifted to rest negligently on the bottom rung of the fence. His hair was short and dark, but thick, as if it would lean towards unruly curls if allowed to grow any longer.

She took in all this in a second, with an accelerating heartbeat. Virile sexuality drenched the air around him like a tangible forcefield and Iseult shivered involuntarily, recognising a base sexuality that seemed to resonate with something equally base within her.

He carried an air of authority and power suited to the monarch he was, ruling over a wealthy sheikhdom where he owned one of the most exclusive thoroughbred stables on the Arabian peninsula. The kind of stables where legendary winners were bred and trained.

With her heart stuttering in her chest, Iseult

watched as the Sheikh calmly and gracefully vaulted over the fence, not a hint of strain on his face even though the fence was over five feet. Immediately Devil's head reared back, nostrils flaring, and he stepped sideways with a skittish move. Iseult patted the horse and murmured encouragement for him to not make this easy on his new owner.

Her father, standing just a few feet away, was sending fervent silent signals to Iseult: *Please behave.* But she was too heartsore to behave, no matter how she'd been momentarily thrown. This man was coolly and calmly taking everything she'd ever known and loved, and there wasn't a thing she could do about it except not make it easy for him.

The Sheikh was looking up at her, and she could see the expressions crossing his face, and his anger mounting that she wasn't jumping off, jumping to attention. While she'd have liked to think that she was consciously making her displeasure known, she knew her inability to move had more to do with his sheer male charisma than any rebellion. Finally her father's voice intruded, and she could hear the fear. 'Iseult, please allow Sheikh Nadim to ride Devil's Kiss. He's come a long way.'

With much less grace than she was used to Iseult slipped off the horse and came around his head to hand the reins to the Sheikh. Her legs turned to water when she recognised just how tall and well built he was. Like one long, lean and hardened muscle, with shoulders so broad they blocked out the background.

She felt innately feminine next to his superior build. It was very disturbing when she'd long ago given up any attempt to explore that side of herself, assuming she just didn't have it in her. Reaction to her thoughts made her all but thrust the reins at him. 'Here you are.'

His black eyes glittered dangerously, and Iseult was glad of the protection of her cap. She desperately wanted him to take the reins before he could see how her hand was starting to shake, and to her intense relief he did. But not before his fingers touched off hers, and she jerked back so quickly that Devil's Kiss moved skittishly again.

Before she could lose it completely she turned and walked away through the soft damp grass, and climbed over the fence jerkily to stand by her father, who was radiating waves of disapproval. She'd never felt so out of control of her own body and emotions, and she didn't like it one bit.

She watched with a thumping heart as Sheikh Nadim coolly and calmly walked around the horse, lengthening the stirrups and running a large brown hand over his flanks. Iseult's belly tightened and she felt a flare of something hot in her abdomen.

Then he vaulted onto the horse with a fluid grace

she'd never seen before, and nudged Devil's Kiss straight into a canter. Iseult's throat dried up completely. Devil's Kiss was an absolute traitor; he'd shown not even a flicker of rebellion at seating this man, clearly recognising his skill and authority.

Sheikh Nadim al Saqr was considered something of a rebel in horse breeding circles, as he'd been slow to set up a base in Europe, preferring to keep his horses in his home country, out of sight and highly secret. The world of flat racing had been sent into a tailspin when he'd entered one of his three-year-olds into the most prestigious race in Europe at Longchamp the previous year and it had won. A rank outsider, who had only raced previously in Dubai, it had stunned everyone and made the racing world sit up and recognise Sheikh Nadim al Saqr as a serious contender.

Beside her, her father chuckled softly and said, 'Weren't expecting Devil's Kiss to take to him like that, were you?'

The backs of Iseult's eyes stung with hot tears, which was so unlike her—after everything she'd been through she rarely if ever resorted to tears, and suddenly she was a bag of weeping hormones. This was the ultimate betrayal, coming on top of everything else. With an incoherent grunt she turned and stormed off, back up the drive to the house they no longer owned, away from the field they also no longer owned.

Her father hissed after her desperately, 'Iseult O'Sullivan, come back here right now. You cannot just walk away—what will he think?'

Iseult turned, but kept walking backwards and flung her arms up. 'We've lost everything, Dad— I'm not going to bow and scrape after that man. Let him take Devil's Kiss back to the stables and scrub him down if he wants him so badly.'

Years of looking after her father and her two younger brothers and sister had put her in a position of unspoken authority in their home. Even her father knew when not to push her; he owed her too much.

It was only then that she noticed the sleek silver Jeep with dark windows and an officious-looking bodyguard standing to attention nearby, intermittently scanning the surroundings from behind black glasses. It made her even angrier, reminding her of the sheer arrogance of his pushy assistant, who'd had the gall to come and look the place over, as if it was a slave girl being sold at an auction, before they'd even publicly announced the sale.

Iseult turned and kept walking, tears blurring her vision. A part of her balked at her extremely uncharacteristic lack of grace and manners, but something about the Sheikh had all her defences raised high and on red alert. She simply couldn't stand there and watch him steal her horse from right under her, and then deal with the undoubtedly arrogant and smug way he'd hand her back the reins as if she was nothing more than a stablehand.

Iseult's tears cleared as she fumed and stomped up the drive; that might be what he was used to in his own country but he wouldn't get away with it here. She imagined him coming from a barbarically foreign place, where he had harems of scantily clad women attending to his every need, and where he lounged on plush velvet and silk cushions in lavish tents in oases in the desert, gorging himself on decadent foods and wines. The man clearly believed himself important enough to merit bringing bodyguards to a quiet and rural part of Ireland.

Her overblown imagination mocked her as she recalled the sliver of hard, olive-skinned, muscle-ridged belly she'd seen as he'd vaulted onto Devil's Kiss, when his shirt had ridden up for a moment. He didn't have the body of a louche decadent, and he didn't strike her as the kind of man who required protecting. Her belly tightened again, and a disturbing pulse throbbed between her legs.

She entered the stableyard and tore off her cap, releasing her hair, breathing hard. Damp sweat pooled uncomfortably between her breasts and trickled down her back. She knew they'd been fighting a losing battle for some time, and that the culmination of it was today. And she knew rationally that she had no real reason to feel such antipathy towards this Sheikh other than the fact he happened to be the new owner…and that he disturbed her on a level she didn't like to think about.

As she looked around the unbearably shabby yard the fight suddenly left her, and she felt overwhelmed with fatigue and grief at seeing all the empty stalls. The stud down the road was equally desolate-looking. The homestead stood to the right of the yard. Once it had gleamed from top to bottom, a grand country house, but now it was a mere shadow of its former self. Everything was peeling and crumbling. She'd worked so hard to try and keep them afloat, but everything had gone against them—not least the global economic crisis.

They might have won two prestigious races recently, but that money had barely made a dent in the huge debts that had built up from years of mismanagement. The one ace up their sleeve had been Devil's Kiss, and now he was gone. Quite literally. The Sheikh had come to transport him to his own country on the Arabian peninsula, where he had plans to train him, race him, and eventually use him to breed even more winners to add to his arsenal. He was going to overhaul their small stud farm and gallops and turn them into something homogenous: a conveyor belt outfit that would 'perform' and meet 'targets', and make a profit and breed winners.

While Iseult had no problem with expansion, and turning their property around so that it functioned properly again on all levels, she'd always loved the fact that they'd remained true to their own identity long after many other farms had sold out to rich Arabs and huge syndicates. Now they were no different from the rest.

Desultorily, Iseult made her way to Devil's Kiss's stable, to get it prepared for his return. She grimaced as she turned on a hose and started to sluice down the yard, thinking of her beloved grandfather, who would have railed against this day too… She'd followed him everywhere until his death; she'd been ten when he'd been struck down with an awful illness and everything had started to unravel…

Iseult diverted her mind away from painful memories. As soon as Devil's Kiss had raced and shown his pedigree as a stunning two-year-old the spotlight had been turned onto their stud—especially as it had been so long since they'd produced a winner. Everyone knew that their backs were against the wall, and that they'd sold all but their oldest mares to concentrate on Devil's Kiss. That buzz was undoubtedly what had brought them to the attention of the Sheikh. And Iseult had to admit bitterly that he'd snapped them up like the bargain they were.

Ridiculously, tears threatened again—too much buried grief swimming up to the surface. And that was when Iseult heard the familiar clatter of hooves in the yard behind her. She hurriedly blinked away her tears and turned around warily to look up. The sun chose that moment to peek out from dark, oppressive clouds and Iseult shivered—because she was momentarily blinded and all she could see was the intimidatingly broad-shouldered silhouette of the Sheikh on Devil's back. Like a portent of doom.

For a second Nadim was utterly transfixed. The girl was revealed fully without that unflattering cap, and she was most definitely a girl—beautiful enough to make his breath catch. Not a scrap of make-up marred her pale alabaster skin and that amazing bone structure. And he'd never seen such unusual colouring: long dark red hair was pulled back into an untidy ponytail which must have been stuffed under the cap, and tendrils drifted and clung to her cheeks and neck. Tight jeans and the fleece did little to disguise the fact that she was tall and slim, lean as a whip, her body sleek and toned.

But it was her eyes that caught him as if spellbound. Huge and almond shaped, with long black

lashes, they were the colour of dark liquid amber.
And as he watched, fascinated, those stunning
eyes flashed a warning and her chest rose and fell,
making him want to drop his gaze and inspect
those delicately feminine swells again. He sensed
instinctively that she was more voluptuous than she
looked, and wondered why she hid her curves. But
he cut off his wandering mind there, when it had
a direct effect on his anatomy. The kick of desire
in his blood made him feel disorientated. It was
unwarranted and completely inappropriate.

Her full mouth had tightened back into the mutinous line. 'If you've quite finished your inspec-
tion, I'll take Devil's Kiss now. I'm not part of the
inventory of your newly acquired assets.'

Her voice was surprisingly husky, but Nadim
didn't dwell on that further enticement now. Her
haughty look forced a surge of anger upward and
drove Nadim off the horse to the ground. Once
again he'd been mesmerised by someone who was
little more than a stablehand. *Unthinkable*. He deliberately ignored her hand, outstretched for the
reins, fixing her with a harsh glare.

It was a struggle for Iseult to stay standing as
the Sheikh came off the horse and stood far too
close for her liking. His slow appraisal just now
had turned her insides to jelly. And now, facing
her like this, he was far more devastating than
she'd acknowledged before. He had to be at least

six foot three and, while she was relatively tall, she felt minute in comparison.

'Correct me if I'm wrong, Miss O'Sullivan, but I believe that you and your father are very much part of the *inventory*. Part of the agreement for the sale of this property outlines the fact that all working staff will be retained to ensure a smooth transition. Are you not part of the staff?'

His deep voice and softly drawled words, with more than a hint of a seductively foreign accent, made Iseult's knees feel curiously weak. Anger at her response made her lash out. 'I'm more than just staff. Perhaps where you come from you're used to buying and selling people, but in this country we've outgrown such antiquated practices.'

His face tightened perceptibly. 'Be very careful, Miss O'Sullivan. You're in danger of going too far. As it is, your insolence is intolerable. I don't appreciate *employees* who talk back or use guard dogs to intimidate.'

Iseult flushed at being reminded of the recent incident with his emissary. 'Murphy isn't a guard dog. He's just protective. Your assistant was trespassing; I was here on my own.'

The Sheikh's mouth was a grim line of displeasure. 'You ignored a perfectly polite request from him to come and see the property even though it was common knowledge you were close to advertising a sale.'

Iseult couldn't meet that blistering dark gaze. She felt about two feet tall. How could she explain to this autocratic man the violently visceral feeling she'd had not to give up and admit defeat? And how his arrogant assistant had effortlessly raised her hackles by being so pushy, making her dread a soulless takeover by a faceless buyer?

He continued, 'Do I need to remind you that very soon I will own everything you see around you, and could have you thrown off this property for good?'

Iseult could feel the colour drain from her face, and saw something flash in his eyes. He even said something that sounded like a curse under his breath and moved towards her. Did he think she was going to faint? Iseult had never fainted in her life. She moved back jerkily, and the Sheikh stopped, his eyes gleaming obsidian.

Nadim had to curb a reflex to apologise—although he couldn't remember the last time he'd had to apologise for anything. He hadn't meant to speak so harshly, but when she'd gone white and looked as if he'd put a knife through her heart his immediate reaction had been one of remorse and to protect. He couldn't believe that this girl had taken him in even for a moment. He allowed no woman to get under his skin so easily.

He shouldn't be demeaning himself by engaging in dialogue with someone like her. She was about to become just one more of hundreds of employees scattered across the globe.

He finally handed her the reins and said curtly, 'Devil's Kiss travels tomorrow. See to it that he's ready.'

CHAPTER TWO

A SHORT while later, her belly still roiling with tangled emotions, Iseult went through the back door into the house, toeing off her boots and muttering under her breath as she walked into the warm and welcoming kitchen, where their housekeeper, Mrs O'Brien, was looking flushed and harried. Their infamous family dog, Murphy, was not doing much to help by getting in her way.

Iseult shooed him out through the door and turned back. 'What's wrong?'

The older woman blew some hair out of her red face. 'Your father informed me barely an hour ago that the Sheikh will have lunch here, along with himself and their solicitors. That's lunch for five people—more than I've had to cook for since the kids went back to college.'

Everyone in the family affectionately referred to Iseult's younger siblings—Paddy Junior, and the twins Nessa and Eoin—as the kids. But now anger bubbled up again to think that the Sheikh, with a mere click of his fingers, was putting them under added pressure. They barely had the money to stock the fridge and cupboards for themselves. Iseult longed to tell Mrs O'Brien to ignore the decree, but she knew her father would die of embarrassment. The fact was, they had no choice but to accept their predicament.

It was the Sheikh or the bank—neither one a palatable option, but at least, Iseult had to concede grudgingly, the Sheikh was keeping her father on as a manager and had offered a decent wage. She didn't like how that concession made her feel guilty now. She knew she'd behaved badly. But right now she didn't want to look at the cause of the irrationality of her response.

Defeatedly she reached for the spare apron and started to help Mrs O'Brien, who sent her a grateful smile as they worked together to bring lunch up to some kind of acceptable standard for a Sheikh.

Carrying a tray of soup starters a short while later, Iseult hesitated at the dining room door for a moment, and had to ignore the shiver of sensation that shot through her body when she heard the low rumble of the Sheikh's sexy voice. *Sexy?* Since when had she been aware of *sexy?* Gritting her teeth and jaw so hard that it hurt, she pasted a bland smile on her face and went in.

Silence greeted her, and she deliberately avoided any eye contact. Her heart ached to see that her father had allowed the Sheikh to sit at the head of the table. Once, in her grandfather's heyday, they had run a hugely successful and thriving business. Renowned horse-breeders from all over the world had come and paid exorbitant sums of money just to have their mares stand at O'Sullivan's stud to be covered by their pure-blooded stallions.

This moment, right now, couldn't make it any clearer how far their fortunes had fallen.

With a shaking hand Iseult served the solicitors their bowls of soup, then her father, and lastly the Sheikh, though she knew she ought to have served him first. Barely holding it together, she somehow managed to grab the tray and go to leave again. But then she heard her father clear his throat.

'Iseult, love, aren't you going to join us?'

She heard the plea in his voice. He depended on her for so much—she was the one who knew the farm inside and out—but in all honesty she hadn't expected to be included in this. Her father remained the public figurehead of the stud despite everything, and Iseult had every hope that one day he'd assume his role fully again. The look in his eyes spoke volumes, though. He was terrified these men would see how little control he had over the place. And he was terrified that they'd renege on the agreement to keep him on as manager.

Iseult hesitated for a second, but then that deep drawling voice came. 'Since when does a stablehand who doubles as a server sit at the table with the new owner? I think not, Mr O'Sullivan. Your daughter can hardly be expected to be party to our private discussions.'

Iseult turned to the Sheikh, the tray still held by her side, and had to restrain the urge not to smash it on his arrogant head. She smiled sweetly, while mentally apologising to her father. She deliberately made her Irish brogue even stronger. 'I couldn't agree more, Sheikh. I know my place. And I've a horse to get ready for the travelling tomorrow— straight after I've finished serving the lunch, of course.'

With that she bobbed a curtsey, and as she left she could have sworn she heard a muffled snigger coming from where their own solicitor had been sitting.

Iseult thought it best to let Mrs O'Brien retrieve the soup bowls and serve the main course. But when she got busy making Irish coffees and asked Iseult to get the plates she couldn't avoid going back.

The silence was thick with tension when she walked into the room, and Iseult's skin prickled under the weight of one particularly heavy gaze. Somehow she managed to take the plates while avoiding all eye contact. She could see that her father's face was slightly flushed, and her belly clenched in an automatic reaction of anxiety. But to her relief she saw that he was still drinking water. He'd been dry for years now, but she knew something like this had the potential to send him back to a dark place. Her conscience struck her hard. She wasn't exactly helping matters.

With all the plates balanced precariously in her arms, Iseult got to the door—only to find that it had closed on her. She had a split second of wondering what to do, and then she felt a large dark presence loom behind her. A tantalising scent of something sensuously foreign tickled her nostrils, making her belly clench again—but this time for a very different reason. In utter surprise, she watched as a tautly muscled brown arm reached around her to open the door.

She had to step back closer to the Sheikh in order for him to open it, and for a very disturbing moment the entire length of her back was pressed against his hard chest and belly. It was like a wall of steel. She nearly dropped every plate, but in a smooth move he ushered her out and pulled the door after them, coming round to stand in front of her. Iseult wanted to avoid his eyes, but drummed up all her courage to meet them.

His voice was low, and tore strips off her. 'I didn't appreciate the ham acting, Miss O'Sullivan. Try a cute move like that again and neither you nor your father will have anything further to do with this place. Your name will be history overnight.

I'm beginning to feel that I've been entirely too generous where your father is concerned, and I have serious doubts about his capability to run this place.'

He continued with a blistering tone. 'I have no idea where your misplaced animosity has sprung from; your farm's demise was not by my hand and we've never met before. I suggest you have a think about that before we meet to talk after lunch.'

The plates trembled ominously in Iseult's hands. She found it hard to think straight. 'What do you mean, *talk*?'

'After just ten minutes of conversation with your father it's become clear that he's no more in control of things around here than that homely housekeeper. It would appear that I have underestimated you, Miss O'Sullivan. You will meet with me in your father's study in one hour and you will explain everything to me.'

With that he brushed past her and went back into the room, shutting the door again with a firm click. She stood motionless for a long moment, her heart hammering, until she heard Mrs O'Brien huffing up the stairs with a tray full of desserts and Irish coffees. In a state of shock, Iseult put down the plates on a nearby table and opened the door for Mrs O'Brien before escaping back to the kitchen. She couldn't have helped give out the desserts even if she'd wanted to. She knew that something hot or cold would have ended up in someone's lap because she was shaking so hard with reaction.

She dumped the plates in a dishwasher that had seen better days, and fled outside after stuffing her feet back into her mucky boots.

Once in the yard, sucking in deep breaths of fresh air, Iseult put her hands to her hot cheeks. What was wrong with her? The Sheikh was absolutely right. It wasn't his fault they were in this position; this had been coming for a long, long time. He'd just taken advantage of their weakness in a challenging market. And, as she'd conceded earlier, being bought out by him was infinitely preferable to being bought out and sold off in pieces by the bank.

So, apart from the heartache of losing their family business, what was wrong with her? She knew more than most people how things changed, and plenty of their neighbours had undergone similar buyouts to survive. In a way, they'd been lucky; thanks to Devil's Kiss they'd survived far longer than anyone had thought they would—long enough to see the kids settled at college in Dublin.

Iseult walked instinctively towards the stables, where Devil's Kiss heard her coming and put his head out over his door with a welcoming whinny. Iseult smiled sadly and went over, rubbing him affectionately on the nose. 'This is our last day together, Devil. You'll be gone tomorrow...'

A huge lump constricted Iseult's throat then, and she fought not to give in to the grief when she thought of how she'd hoped and prayed for a different outcome. But one good horse could never have turned their fortunes around. They'd have needed ten winners for that. Everyone had depended on her for as long as she could remember, so it was second nature now to bottle it up, swallow the lump down.

Her thoughts gravitated back to the Sheikh, and how threatened she'd felt just now with his tall, hard body against her back. She shivered. She couldn't explain it, but from the moment she'd heard he was coming to get Devil's Kiss himself her hackles had risen for no good reason. She'd put it down to the fact that she'd have felt that way about whoever the new owner was, but it was almost as if some sixth sense had warned her that he would threaten her on many more levels than that of just being the new owner of their stud, which was ridiculous.

Her conscience struck her again; she'd felt that way as soon as she'd seen the pictures of him on the internet. It had been a physical reaction to his image that had no basis in logic or rationality. She'd never been one to sigh over and lust after pin-ups; those normal rites of passage were something she'd never had time to indulge in as a teenager.

But then today her fears had been confirmed.

From the moment she'd seen him out of the corner of her eye as she'd exercised Devil's Kiss on the gallops every sense had gone onto high alert. Which had only got worse when she'd actually seen him up close. He was hard and implacable. Unreadable. And yet…some deeply secret and feminine part of her had *thrilled* inside when she'd seen him in the flesh.

Her mouth compressed as she continued to rub Devil's Kiss distractedly. After losing her mother at the tender age of twelve, she'd never had anyone to encourage her out of her naturally tomboyish state. Her one failed attempt to be feminine had ended in abject humiliation, after which she'd vowed never to let anyone make her feel so vulnerable again…

Iseult cursed herself now. *Why* was she thinking of that memory? An image of the Sheikh's hard, beautiful face came into her mind and her belly quivered. She resolutely refused to acknowledge the fact that this complete stranger seemed to have unlocked something deeply feminine within her, bringing back painful memories. It was preposterous, because there was no way on this earth that a man like him would ever notice someone like her. She'd seen pictures of his women on the internet: all stunning, polished, *gorgeous*. Everything Iseult wasn't and never would be.

She turned and walked back to the house

reluctantly, driving down the mounting feeling of dread at the thought of facing the Sheikh again. She would have to apologise to him for her behaviour.

After taking off her boots again, and replacing them with trainers in the room beside the kitchen, Iseult walked through the house and paused outside the study door. Taking a deep breath, she knocked lightly and went in.

The Sheikh stood looking out of the big window which took in a view of rolling green fields as far as the eye could see and the gallops in the distance. Iseult's breath hitched and her heart took up an unsteady rhythm. And then he slowly turned around, and heat climbed up her chest and into her face.

She stayed near the door and saw one ebony brow arch imperiously. She was reminded in that instance who she was dealing with, and who she had trifled with. She swallowed. 'I owe you an apology.'

The brow stayed arched. He wasn't going to make this easy.

'I'm sorry if I gave you the impression that I was—'

He cut in then, and she could hear the anger vibrating in his voice. 'Rude? Obnoxious? Behaving like a petulant teenager?'

Iseult fought to clamp down on a renewed surge

of anger and clenched her fists. The Sheikh walked over to sit against the huge desk, crossing his arms over that formidable chest. In her peripheral vision Iseult could see the material of his jeans straining over his powerful thighs, and for a dizzy second she forgot what he'd just said.

But then she remembered. Her vision cleared, the red mist lifted. She lifted her chin. 'I'm apologising now for my behaviour. I had no right to treat you with such disrespect.'

'No, you didn't.' He sounded a little surprised, and looked at her assessingly. 'But I can appreciate that this must be a difficult situation, so I'm prepared to give you the benefit of the doubt. For now.'

His eyes dropped for a moment, in a long sweep down her body. Iseult could feel that clammy sweat break out again. Why did she feel as if he'd undressed her every time he did that?

'After all,' he drawled, his eyes on hers again, 'you can't be more than…what? Eighteen?'

That red mist hovered close again. Iseult had to will it down and bit out, 'I'm no child. I'm twenty-three.'

Nadim had to quell the surge of reaction when he heard how old she was. She was the same age as Sara had been when she'd— He ruthlessly cut off his thoughts there, uncomfortably aware of how different the woman in front of him was from his late wife. He didn't appreciate being reminded of her now, and it made his voice harsh.

'Clearly a very immature twenty-three-year-old, who can't abide the thought of no longer being the mistress of the house.'

Iseult felt hysteria rising. '*Clearly* you've not taken a close look at your new property, Sheikh. It's been a long time since there was a mistress of this house the way you're implying. Everyone here works day and night to keep the place running. Even Mrs O'Brien hasn't been paid in months; she's here out of loyalty and because we provide a roof over her head.' Her voice took on a bitter edge. 'But evidently sheer hard work wasn't enough to bring us through tough times.'

'Or a good horse…' Nadim said.

'Or a good horse,' Iseult repeated, unable to hide the weariness in her voice.

Nadim was taken aback by the sudden jump from passion to defeat. He'd clearly hit a nerve. Taking a closer look for the first time, he could see that Iseult was actually bordering on being painfully thin. And when her face wasn't flushed with anger, as he'd seen it often enough today, it was pale…too pale. He could see faint purple shadows under her eyes. Something shifted in his chest, and a protective instinct nearly overwhelmed him with its force.

'Is your father still drinking?' he asked then, so

abruptly that Iseult's face flushed again. Curiously, it made Nadim feel somehow comforted.

She shook her head fiercely, her eyes flashing a warning. 'He hasn't touched a drop in seven years. And he won't—ever again.'

Nadim's mouth quirked, but not with humour. 'Not even you can guarantee that—and I saw your worried glance earlier, before you saw he was drinking water. How do you know this transition won't send him off the rails again? After all, isn't that what precipitated your decline?'

Iseult wondered dimly how he'd so effortlessly articulated her own innermost worries, how he knew so much, but then had to concede that her father's drinking problem had been common knowledge within their circles—despite her attempts to hide it and take his workload onto her shoulders.

Reluctantly she explained, 'We started to do badly when my grandfather became gravely ill— nearly thirteen years ago. We'd had a run of bad luck…disappointing foals and yearlings. The owners of the horses we were training got nervous after my grandfather died and sent them to other trainers.'

Her mouth twisted. 'We were suddenly *un-fashionable*. And we were up against much more successful studs with infinitely more resources than we had. Not long after my grandfather died my mother passed away, and that was when my father…'

She didn't have to finish. She couldn't finish. In truth, she was a little stunned that she'd just shared what she had. But some instinct had warned her that the Sheikh would dig until he got to the very bottom of their *modus operandi* and how they'd got to this dismal state of affairs. And if he went through the paperwork it wouldn't take him long to trace events back to her grandfather's death, and then her mother's.

He was frowning at her now. 'What happened then? Who did your father bring in to keep this place running?'

Iseult shook her head, feeling shame mount for the first time in her life at hearing their history articulated so baldly. At knowing that she had failed. 'No one. We all pulled together. I…' She faltered, and then hitched her chin again. 'I helped until my father could get back on his feet again…and since I left school I've been working here full-time.'

There was no expression on the Sheikh's face, but Iseult could see a muscle pulse in his jaw. 'Your brothers and sisters?'

'I've two brothers and one sister. They're away in college in Dublin. They helped out when they could.'

Nadim reeled inwardly. At the mere age of twelve she had taken on that burden, along with school? If what Iseult was saying was true, then she'd more or less single-handedly helped keep the stables afloat. He could tell that she was embarrassed, and he could also tell that she was used to protecting her father. He felt a surge of anger towards that man now, and couldn't fathom how his perception of this woman before him had changed so much in such a short space of time.

'And Devil's Kiss? You trained him?'

Iseult flushed. 'With my father. We both did.'

Nadim felt on a more even keel here. 'How do you know that you haven't overtrained him? That he isn't peaking too early?'

Sheer pride straightened Iseult's back. 'Do *you* think he's peaking too early? Couldn't you tell just from riding him today that if anything his winning those races was just a sign of things to come?'

Her confidence astounded him, but he had to admit grudgingly to himself that he had formed that opinion. 'You're very confident.'

'Because I know horses, and I know Devil's Kiss. He's not yet shown half his potential. His lineage is pure thoroughbred; his father was Hawk Eye and his dam was Sheila's Wish, whose line goes back directly to Queen of Tara.'

Nadim knew Devil's Kiss's stellar lineage back to front, and Iseult was right. 'If what you say is true...you do know what you're saying?'

Iseult nodded. 'He could become something very special.'

'More than special—a world champion.'

Iseult nodded again, surprised to recognise that he was hearing her and taking her opinion on board. She'd chafed to think that he didn't rate her training skills. While she knew she had a long way to go, she'd always had the confidence instilled within her from her grandfather to trust her instincts. And she knew she was right when it came to Devil's Kiss.

The Sheikh stood from the desk then, and in a skittish move Iseult took a step back—even though feet separated them. She caught his dark look and cursed herself for reacting, hating that he might suspect she was so aware of him. She watched as he walked around the desk and sat down in the high-backed leather chair that had been her grandfather's.

He gestured her forward to take the seat on the other side. Too hot inside, and bemused, Iseult couldn't even feel insulted that he was clearly taking control. When she'd sat down, he flicked a hand over a sheaf of papers on the desk.

'The papers are signed, Iseult. I now own everything.' His dark look speared her. 'I now own *you*.'

Iseult's throat dried up. She was reacting to too many things at once. The fact that he'd just called her by her name, with that deep voice and sexy accent making it sound deliciously foreign and sensual, and also—despite her assertion earlier that she wasn't part of the inventory—the fact she couldn't refute his claim that he owned her. She was as much a part of this place as the earth of the land and the stones of the house. She'd even been born in her parents' bedroom upstairs.

'So...?' she managed to croak out. 'What...?'

Nadim looked at the young woman opposite him. He didn't like to acknowledge how hearing how old she was had seemed to make his awareness of her increase thousandfold within him—as if he'd been denying it to himself when he'd believed her to be out of bounds.

And she still was. Yet, despite that assertion, he knew what he wanted with stunning clarity—and what he wanted was to keep this woman close, for such myriad reasons that he wasn't even going to investigate them now. He made a split-second decision.

'A chain of events has been set into motion. This will become my European base. It will need to be built up. As you may already know, I've acquired the land adjoining the stud down the road...'

Iseult nodded in acknowledgement. It had been the first sign of how determined he was to buy them out. He'd been so confident of acquiring their stud that he'd invested in the land around them before they'd even announced the sale. Her anger at his arrogance had surged from that point. But, in fairness, she could see now that it would have been directed at anyone who had stepped in to buy them out...

'I've already hired a new manager to come in and take over both facilities—the training grounds and the stud—'

Iseult gasped, pulled out of her straying thoughts. 'I thought you were going to allow my father to stay on.' Anger blurred her vision. For a second there she'd been distracted by this man's sheer charisma, when all along— 'If you think that you can come in here like this and just—'

He surged up from his seat to place both hands on the desk, and towered over Iseult in the chair. '*Stop* talking—right now.'

Her heart nearly jumped out of her chest, and along with shock at his quick anger Iseult also felt a dangerous thrill at being so close to that vibrant, tightly coiled energy.

He sat back down and raked a hand through his hair, impatience bouncing off him in waves. 'You are unbelievably impertinent. No one speaks to me like this—*no one*. The fact that you are even here, having this conversation with me, is because I recognise the role you have played here. That is *all*. Believe me, in any other instance you would be lucky to have me acknowledge your existence—never mind conduct a discourse like this.'

Iseult clamped her mouth shut on the words aching to trip off her tongue at his arrogance. In truth, he was intimidating her more than she cared to admit, and after seeing the evidence of his protective entourage she could well imagine that he wouldn't normally have cast someone like her a second glance. The thought surprisingly sank like a lead balloon in her belly.

'Your father *is* being kept on—exactly as I promised. But in an advisory capacity at first. I will *not* allow someone to take over the running of this place who has so obviously let it slip between his fingers. And, despite your noble defence of him, I'm not convinced that his weakest traits are behind him.'

Iseult could feel herself blanch. He meant her father's drinking. She couldn't meet the Sheikh's eyes for long, feeling as if he was looking right into her soul and seeing her own private fears laid bare. Because she wasn't entirely sure herself how her father would react.

'My newly appointed manager will start here tomorrow, early, and I expect you to give him a full rundown of everything. I know you still have some mares. The fact that you have a training facility here at the house is one of your great advantages, making this a fully sufficient stud, which is exactly what I want to expand upon. Then will come the task of acquiring new foals, yearlings, stallions and mares, and slowly building everything from the ground up again...'

Iseult nodded her head, a tiny spark of excitement spiking through her to think of them getting an overhaul and breeding once again. 'I can fill the new manager in when he comes...we'll have some time, though, won't we? The autumn yearling sales won't be starting for a few weeks.'

Nadim just looked at her, and Iseult felt something unspoken move between them. Instinctively she shivered.

'*He* will have plenty of time, yes. Along with your father. You, however, will have just the morning to acquaint him with everything you've dealt with. Because tomorrow early evening you'll be travelling to Merkazad with Devil's Kiss.'

CHAPTER THREE

ISEULT just looked at the Sheikh dumbly. She shook her head faintly. '*Merkazad?* What's Merkazad? I'll be needed here.'

His face tightened ominously, 'Merkazad is where I live—my country. It's a small independent sheikhdom in the southern region of Al-Omar. And, yes, you are coming.'

Fear made her heart stop. 'But *why*? Why would you need me to come there? You have a veritable industry in your own country.'

He arched his brow again. 'You've been checking me out?'

Iseult flushed, mortified. 'I just looked you up to see who our new owner was, that's all.' Except now all she could think of were those pictures of his glamorous women.

Nadim couldn't really believe he was still having this conversation. He *told* people what he wanted and they obeyed. It was simple and straightforward and had been all his life. But for the first time it wasn't. And it came in the shape of this redhaired, quick-tempered woman before him, who was still dressed in the clothes she'd worn when riding Devil's Kiss earlier.

He looked at her mouth, which was as lusciously full and sensuous as he'd suspected it would be when he'd first seen her, and felt a flash of desire in that moment so strong that he had to clench a fist against his thigh under the desk. He questioned his sanity at insisting she come to his country, but something compelling wouldn't allow him to backtrack.

He gritted out words through that unbidden and unwelcome wave of desire. 'You will be coming to Al-Omar, and then on to Merkazad. There will be no further discussion on this.'

As if his words had finally broken through her shock at his announcement, Iseult stood up jerkily from the chair and spun away into the room. She put out a hand, as if that could encompass everything.

'But I can't just leave here. This is my home. I've been working here for ever.' She could feel hysteria rising as it all hit her at once—the magnitude of what he was saying. 'My father—how will he cope without me? And the kids? I'm all they have. I can't just leave them behind—'

The Sheikh had stood too, his whole body taut with obvious anger that she persisted in defying him. '*Who,*' he barked out, frowning fiercely, 'are *the kids*? Don't tell me you have a brood of children up your sleeve that your father omitted to mention?'

Nadim didn't know why that sudden thought made his vision blur with incandescence—so much so that he barely saw Iseult shaking her head forcibly.

'No—*no*, of course I have no children. I'm talking about my brothers and sister. Since Mum died I'm all they've had.'

Nadim's vision cleared. He was surprised to find that he was so angry, and so *relieved*. He moved around the desk to the other side, further enraged at seeing how Iseult backed away. Her hair had all but unravelled from her ponytail, and long tendrils curled like dark flames around her slim shoulders.

He forced himself to keep his eyes on her face and ignore the banking desire within him, still astounded that she was having this effect on him. It had to be some arbitrary reaction because he'd not taken a new mistress in months. Sheer sexual frustration, that was all. A physical response to an attractive woman.

'You said they were all in college.'

'They are…' Iseult desperately tried to appeal to this man. 'But the twins are just eighteen years old. They've never lived away from home before.'

'Their home isn't going anywhere,' Sheikh Nadim pointed out curtly. 'I've been more than generous in allowing your family to remain here.'

'No,' said Iseult, feeling guilty again, knowing how different things would be if they'd been facing a takeover by the bank, 'but if I'm not here... they...'

Even as she said the words she could recognise how pathetic they sounded. She knew very well that Paddy Junior was fine and most likely not coming home until Christmas time, and the twins were in the same college, happily set up in on-campus accommodation with other schoolfriends who were doing the same course. Iseult had settled them in herself, just last week.

'When I was eighteen I'd already travelled the world on my own—*twice.*'

Iseult took in the arrogant look on the Sheikh's face. Her blood boiled ominously again. 'You come from a very different part of the world—'

'Not so different. I was educated in England.' His voice was dry as toast. 'Not around a campfire in the desert, as you might imagine. And yet I took off as soon as I tasted my chance of independence. Your siblings are grown-ups and you are not their mother.'

Iseult flushed at having her prejudice pointed out to her and choked back the need to say, *But I have been their mother.* Ridiculously, she felt tears threaten. Her responsibility to her family was so ingrained she felt as though she truly *was* a mother being asked to turn her back on her children.

Before she could say anything, though, Sheikh Nadim continued bitingly, 'I know very well what it's like. I lost both my parents at a young age and had to take responsibility for not only my own younger brother but also for my country. It will do your siblings good to know that you won't always be here for them, and it will do your father good to step into his role more fully. *He* will be here if they need him.'

Somehow Iseult managed to swallow back her emotion, recognising on some level the merit in what Sheikh Nadim said, while also being intrigued at the glimpse into his own personal history, of which there had been very little on the internet. The unexpected empathy she felt blindsided her momentarily.

'But…what would I do in…in Merkazad?'

'You will become part of my staff. Initially you will work at the stables, and in time I may allow you to stay involved in Devil's Kiss's training— once I'm confident of your ability. My ambition is to race him as a three-year-old in the Prix de l'Arc next year, with a view to the Dubai World Cup the year after, so my main concern now is that he's not peaking too early.'

Despite the fact that her world was being up-ended around her, Iseult felt a quiver of excitement deep in her belly at knowing that she was being offered the chance to stay near Devil's Kiss. This man, after all, was the man who had thrown the racing fraternity into disarray just last year, and he had a growing reputation as a thoroughbred owner, breeder and trainer to be matched with the best in the world. But even so what he was saying was too huge to process. Still she resisted. 'What if I refuse to go?'

Sheikh Nadim strolled towards her then, and she had to fight every impulse to run. She stayed standing in front of him. He stopped just mere feet away and she looked up, her throat drying again in acknowledgement of his sheer height and powerful build. That too-beautiful face with its harsh lines. It made her think of the desert and wonder how he'd look in that environment.

Nadim reacted forcibly to something deep within him not to give Iseult any way out other than *his* way. 'It's quite simple, Iseult. If you refuse to go then you will be escorted off this property for good. If you refuse then I won't have you working for me in any capacity.'

'You can't do that,' she blustered, desperately scared that he *could*. 'My father would still be here.'

'I could arrange for that to be otherwise. Like

I've said before, I'm still not convinced he will be an asset to this stud.'

Iseult had a horrible vision of her brothers and sister being told that they'd lost their home. She rushed to a quick defence. 'My father is a brilliant trainer. He's just been through a difficult time, that's *all*. He just couldn't—'

She stopped. She'd already said too much. Sheikh Nadim filled in the gap when he said with deceptive softness, '*Cope?* Is that the word you're looking for?'

Iseult's eyes felt gritty, but she refused to be too intimidated to look this man in the eye. Her voice quivered with passion. 'My father is a good man and he knows his business inside out. He taught me everything I know, and he will turn this stud around…with help. All he needs is a chance.'

Sheikh Nadim seemed to ignore her last words. 'Was he the one who taught you to be so wilful?'

Iseult bristled. 'Where I'm from women are encouraged to be independent and to have an opinion and not be scared of sharing it. I'm sorry if you're not used to that.'

Nadim smiled mockingly. 'I don't think you're sorry at all. I think you'll find that women in my country are encouraged to do exactly the same thing—' here his eyes ran her up and down and clearly found her lacking '—but they go about it in a rather more genteel way.'

Iseult's fists clenched, emotion surging easily again. What was it about this man? He seemed to have taken control of some inner emotional barometer she'd never been aware of before. She'd never felt so conscious of her tomboyish state as she did now, and deep down in the very centre of her anger was a secretly treacherous desire to be as genteel as those women Sheikh Nadim spoke of with such respect in his voice. She hated him even more for making her feel like that.

Every righteous bone in her body quivered. 'So my only option is to go and work for you, or face being thrown off this land that has been in my family for generations?'

Nadim's jaw hardened. He had to consciously *not* give in to the compelling need to force this woman to bend to his will. 'I think you'll find that you're being offered an opportunity that many would give their right arm to experience.' This was said with not a little arrogance. 'And you do have a choice, Iseult. There's a whole world out there. I'm not stopping you from leaving to seek employment elsewhere. I'm sure with your experience and crude training ability you'll find a job soon enough—and who knows? You might even become a trainer of some recognition some day.'

Iseult opened her mouth with a hot response,

but Sheikh Nadim put up a hand to stop her. Her mouth closed ineffectually.

'But if you come to my stables you'll have the chance to be taught by the best in the business. And if and when you do return here to work, it would be beneficial for you to know how I run my stables and stud. You would also have the chance to see Devil's Kiss mature into the greatness we both believe he has within him. Can you walk away from that?'

A sense of inevitability washed through Iseult. Of course she couldn't walk away from that. Devil's Kiss was the last in a long line of horses they had owned and bred themselves—the last of her grandfather's legacy. They'd had to sell all the others off just to survive.

She'd nurtured Devil's Kiss like her own baby, and the thought of not seeing him come to fruition after showing such promise was too painful to contemplate. It hurt to recognise the fact that if not for this man she could very well have been waving goodbye to Devil's Kiss the following day, only being allowed to follow his progress second-hand in the papers or on the internet. She might also have been facing the prospect of leaving her house and home too—for good.

All she had to do was sacrifice her own desire to remain here, and that would keep her father, the kids and Mrs O'Brien safe and secure. How could she not do that? How could she deny Mrs O'Brien the chance to receive a wage again after months of working for just board and food?

Her fears had stemmed from hearing stories of other rich buyers coming and firing countless lifelong employees, only to instal their own hand-picked staff. That had been one of the reasons for Iseult's fierce antipathy to this buyout: the fear of the same happening. But it wasn't. Sheikh Nadim was, as he'd already pointed out, being more than generous, and if Iseult wasn't careful she would be the one to sabotage everything.

She lifted her gaze from somewhere to the left of Sheikh Nadim's shoulder and looked him in the eye. Some little stone of resistance within her made her ask, 'Why are you doing this? I mean, why aren't you just letting us all go?'

The Sheikh's dark eyes glittered dangerously, and Iseult had the feeling that not many people questioned anything he did. His jaw clenched, but he answered tightly, 'Because I know what it's like to have everything you know jeopardised. I'm aware this is a relatively small community, and I don't really want to start on the wrong footing by having your neighbours reluctant to do business with me out of loyalty to your father. I also don't see the merit in letting your father or housekeeper go when they know the lie of this land. As it is, retaining them is worth more to me than the money I'll be paying them.'

His face hardened then, and Iseult shivered.

'But, having said that, I'm also aware that it won't do too much damage in the long run to bring in new staff. So, Iseult, what's it to be? My patience is wearing very thin.'

Iseult knew she really didn't have a choice if she didn't want to risk her family's security or be cast out of her own home for ever. She was aware on some dim level that yet again it was falling to her to take responsibility, but that was eclipsed by her curiosity to know more about his personal history.

Iseult had been avoiding his eyes, but now looked at him. 'How long do you expect me to stay in Merkazad?'

His eyes flashed that warning that was already becoming familiar. 'You will stay for as long as I wish it.'

You will stay for as long as I wish it. His words were so arrogant…so implacable—so ridiculously autocratic in this modern environment. And yet in that moment Iseult felt uncharacteristically powerless to defy him. Mentally she took a deep breath, feeling as if she was stepping into a deep, dark void. 'Very well. I'll travel to Al-Omar with you and Devil's Kiss tomorrow.'

Sheikh Nadim smiled a mocking smile, and

an infuriating glint of triumph lit his eyes. 'Oh, you won't be travelling with me. I'll be leaving as soon as the new manager gets here in the morning. You'll travel with the horse. And I'll expect him to arrive in as good condition as he is right now.'

With that, as if he hadn't just whirled through Iseult's world like an angry tornado, ripping everything apart in its path, he flicked a glance at his expensive-looking watch and said, 'If you'll excuse me, I've got a function to attend in Dublin this evening, and a helicopter waiting to take me back to my hotel. I've made arrangements for Devil's Kiss's travel, and a plane will be ready and waiting. One of my own vets will meet you in the morning and travel with you. I trust you'll have everything you need ready to travel tomorrow?'

Iseult cursed the fact that she couldn't turn around and say that she had no current passport—after all, she'd never been further than England—but all she could do was nod her head and say, 'I'll be ready.'

Late the following morning, as Nadim's plane took off from Dublin Airport, he looked out of the window. But the rolling green fields and the city disappearing underneath couldn't distract him from the one face and one body that he couldn't get out of his mind. It was as if her image had been burnt there with a brand.

Iseult O'Sullivan. A slip of a girl. He could remember the tremor that had run through her body when he'd stood so close behind her in the dining room—how his blood had boiled and he'd wanted to knock the plates out of her arms and snake an arm around her waist and pull her back against him.

His body tightened, and his mouth compressed with anger—at himself. And that anger surged when he recalled how he'd blithely told her things that he'd never discussed even with close aides. The fact that he'd lost his parents as a teenager was common knowledge if you went looking for it, but not something he ever mentioned—*or* the fact that he knew how it felt to have everything he'd taken for granted ripped asunder… And yet with her the words had tripped off his tongue as if he'd been injected with some kind of truth serum.

He should be leaving her here. It made sense on many levels. But what had he done? Ensured that she would be a constant presence and a thorn in his side by insisting that she come to Merkazad with the horse.

Why had he done it?

Her image, the way she'd sat so imperiously on the horse when he'd first seen her blazed into his imagination in an eloquent answer.

He thought of the way she'd stood before him so defiantly the day before, and how he'd had to struggle to remember his train of thought when his mind had melted in a haze of lust at imagining revealing her breasts, to see if she hid them as he suspected she did. He shook his head now, as if that could dislodge her image from the gnarled heat in his blood.

He reassured himself that he'd been right to insist that she come to Merkazad. He did want to ensure a smooth transition for Devil's Kiss, and the horse was clearly attached to her. She was also wilful and independent, and had obviously grown far too used to running the business with disastrous consequences. The girl was a liability, and could do with being taught the proper way of things. He could no more leave a loose cannon like her here than he could blithely allow her father to retain complete control.

Nadim felt himself relax. He was merely protecting his new venture by keeping Iseult O'Sullivan where he could see her. He had full confidence that when he touched down on his own familiar soil—*home*—and saw her in his environment, the spell she'd cast over him would dissipate like the mirage of an oasis in the desert. He ruthlessly ignored the *frisson* of something that felt awfully like erotic anticipation when he thought of seeing her at his own stables, against the backdrop of his own rocky and austere land.

He was used to being in control of his desire

for women, that was all, and she'd taken him by surprise. *That was all.* He'd learnt the most tragic of lessons not so long ago. Emotions and women were a fatal mix. Since then his life had been about logic and clear reason.

He refused to believe that his life was deviating in any way from the clear and controlled lines he'd grown used to.

Iseult blinked and breathed in the warm and very foreign air. They'd arrived at a small airfield in Al-Omar just a short time before, and while the vet was checking Devil's Kiss in the specially modified hold of the private jet Iseult had stepped out onto the tarmac, already too hot in her slim parka jacket.

It was night, so she couldn't see much, but she felt the residue of a very hot day settle around her shoulders like a warm cloak. The sky was a dark indigo colour, and a crescent moon hung suspended on its back, as if knocked from the sideways perch she'd grown used to seeing it take all her life. Stars glittered so close and clear she felt as if she could reach out and touch one.

Just then she heard a noise, and saw a couple of sleek dark Jeeps driving across the tarmac to greet them—one with a horsebox attached. They stopped, and Iseult's heart stopped too. Would *he* be here to meet her? It scared her slightly, how her heart leapt at that thought and her throat dried in anticipation.

But when the Jeeps came to a stop and she didn't see him emerge she immediately felt silly. Of course he wouldn't come to meet her. She was just an employee now. Some official-looking men got out of the vehicle without the horsebox and she looked to them.

Nadim hesitated before he got out of his Jeep. Iseult O'Sullivan stood on the tarmac looking unbelievably vulnerable, and even from here he could see the shadows of fatigue under her huge eyes. Her hair was back in that untidy ponytail.

She'd been cool and contained that morning when he'd come to the farm, studiously avoiding his eyes and concentrating on the new manager. Her reluctance to leave her home had been tangible. Something twisted in Nadim's gut now, and he cursed the impulse which had led him first of all to bring her here, and now to come and collect her himself. The last thing he needed was to be feeling inordinately protective over a new employee.

He'd told himself that it made complete sense for him to meet Iseult and Devil's Kiss himself. But his head groom Jamilah's eloquent silence had spoken volumes when he'd told her what he was doing. She hadn't needed to spell out that he'd never done this before—especially when *she* was usually the one to meet new horses and bring them to the stables.

Iseult was watching the uniformed men approach her and starting to feel very alone and very conscious of the fact that she was in a foreign land with not one person she knew anywhere near. What if they didn't speak English? What if they weren't expecting her? But just then she felt a prickling on the back of her neck, and heard the sound of a door opening from the other Jeep.

Her head whipped round and her heart stuttered to a stop as she saw the impossibly tall and broad figure of Sheikh Nadim uncoil from the vehicle. He was dressed all in black, and looked so ridiculously gorgeous and exotic that Iseult felt weakness invade her limbs. She told herself it wasn't abject relief at seeing him there.

He strode over to where she stood, and Iseult was rendered speechless. At his brusque, 'I trust you had a pleasant flight?' she just nodded helplessly.

He gestured then to the men in uniform, who had stopped a respectful distance away. 'These men are from Immigration in Al-Omar and Merkazad. They'll check through your documents and issue you with the work visa that I've organised.'

Iseult's head was spinning as she murmured something that she hoped was coherent. This wasn't what she'd been expecting at all, and being faced with Sheikh Nadim like this was making treacherous butterflies erupt in her belly. It was very disturbing to know that this man had completely upended her life in the space of thirty-six hours, and what she felt for him had morphed from intense antipathy and mistrust to something much more nebulous and scary.

In no time at all the smiling men had handed Iseult back her passport, which was now covered with various official-looking stamps. Sheikh Nadim was with the vet and leading Devil's Kiss out of the hold, down a ramp.

He looked at Iseult as she approached. 'He fared well through the journey?'

Iseult looked to the vet for confirmation. He nodded his head. 'Yes, he was fine.'

'That's good news,' Sheikh Nadim said. 'Sometimes if a horse does not weather its first air journey well, it's an indication of problems.'

Iseult was trying to ignore the persistent feeling of relief—and also the way Nadim's big graceful hands, smoothing over Devil's Kiss's flanks, was making her feel hot inside.

Together they installed Devil's Kiss in the most luxurious horsebox Iseult had ever seen, and after saying goodnight to the vet Sheikh Nadim made sure Iseult's luggage was installed before they got into the Jeep.

It was only as they were driving out of the airfield that Iseult noticed two other similar Jeeps come into position—one before them and one behind them. She guessed that they must be his bodyguards. It was only then that she saw all the Jeeps had ceremonial flags attached on either side of the bonnets, reminding her of the status of the man beside her.

Once they were on a well-lit and sleek-looking motorway, Iseult said nervously, 'I wasn't expecting to see you at the airfield.'

Sheikh Nadim flicked her a cursory glance and said coolly, 'I had a meeting with the Sultan of Al-Omar, but he got called away on sudden business so I decided to return home tonight. I have a meeting in Merkazad in the morning that I don't want to miss.'

Iseult's hands twisted in her lap. Of course he hadn't come to meet her out of anything other than pure practical necessity.

She was acutely aware of the Sheikh's huge rangy body beside hers in the luxury Jeep, and was so tense she nearly jumped out of her skin when he said, 'You'll have time to rest and settle in once we get to my stables. I won't expect you to start to work straight away.'

Iseult looked at Nadim, taking in his harsh but beautiful profile. Being taken out of her comfort zone so spectacularly was making her feel intensely vulnerable. 'It has been a bit of a whirlwind… This isn't exactly what I was expecting.'

He inclined his head. 'My head groom is called Jamilah. She'll show you around in the morning and tell you how things run. It'll be up to her as to how she sees fit to use you.'

Iseult was taking this information in, and her silence must have sent a message to Sheikh Nadim, who sent her a mocking glance. 'You weren't expecting that I'd employ a female head groom?'

Iseult flushed and said defensively, 'It's not that common. Even in Ireland it's more usual to find stables largely run by men.'

'You'll find that women are widely employed in all kinds of jobs in Merkazad—although outside the main towns and cities things are still more conservative and traditional. If anything, we try to cling onto that. It's a pity the more traditional nomadic Bedu way of life is becoming a thing of the past. The Bedu warriors are the ancestors of my people. Merkazad has always been a defensive stronghold.'

Despite her tiredness, Iseult was suddenly fascinated to know more. But she felt too shy to ask, and instead just asked how far they were from Merkazad.

'Our journey won't take long. Ordinarily we would fly my horses into B'harani, the capital of Al-Omar, but it adds a couple of hours onto the journey. Sometimes we use that airfield, which is closer to the Merkazad border. We're in the process of building an airstrip and a small airport in northern Merkazad, but it won't be ready for at least another year.'

'Oh...' Iseult fell silent and looked out at the impenetrable darkness outside, wondering what lay beyond. Was it desert? She'd seen them cross over the Arabian Sea as they'd flown in to land, so they weren't far from the coast. She'd read up on Merkazad last night on the internet, and had learnt that it was tiny—literally just about one hundred miles from north to south, and two hundred miles from east to west. It had a natural border of a mountain range within Al-Omar, and had been ruled by Sheikh Nadim's father before his death some twenty years before, when it had passed to Nadim.

The little information apart from that had told her how it had been fought over for many years by various rulers of Al-Omar, before Sheikh Nadim and the current Sultan of Al-Omar had reached a momentous peace agreement fifteen years ago. Iseult had realised that Nadim must have been only about twenty-one then, and had felt stunned to think of someone that young taking on such responsibility.

They were climbing into the mountains now, and Nadim explained to Iseult, 'Once we're through the mountains the altitude drops again. The country literally sits within them, almost like a plateau. It'll probably surprise you when you see it if you're expecting a desert. We have our own ecosystem, thanks to the geography, and we're the only region that experiences a monsoon. We've just come out of it, so the land is still relatively lush.'

Before long Iseult could feel that they were indeed driving down, and within the hour she finally saw lights ahead. She was reminded of footage she'd seen on TV of what it was like to approach Las Vegas in the desert at night.

There were no skyscrapers or buildings taller than two or three storeys, but everything glittered and looked very clean. It was late, so not many people were on the streets. A beautifully ornate mosque was floodlit against the night sky and stars. The architecture of the buildings was a mix between something very Arabic and also something much more European, and she recalled reading in its history of a brief invasion led by colonising Portuguese. The roads were wide and straight, with tall palm trees swaying gently in the night breeze.

Not long after driving through the intriguing city and into a more suburban area Sheikh Nadim turned onto a long winding road which eventually led to a white-walled compound where a lit-up sign read *al Saqr Stables*. The huge heavy gates opened slowly and the Jeeps filed in.

Iseult's eyes opened in wonder as the interior was revealed. A massive courtyard held all sorts of vehicles: horseboxes, Jeeps and cars. There was an enormous green grassy area, where a water fountain shot high in the air, falling down in a glittering cascade into an ornate pool.

Two wide driveways appeared to lead away from the courtyard, and while the bodyguards' Jeeps parked up, and Iseult saw huge burly men emerge, Nadim kept driving and took the right-hand fork.

'I'm taking you to the staff accommodation area, which is beside the main stables. One of the grooms will meet us there and take Devil's Kiss to his new box.'

Iseult was beginning to feel light-headed, and she wasn't sure if it was from fatigue, delayed shock, or just the effect of Sheikh Nadim. She realised that not once since she'd arrived had she thought of home or her family.

Meeting the new manager that morning, and seeing the way he'd listened so patiently to her father, had made her feel inordinately relieved. She'd been even more relieved to hear that he too was committed to a vision of keeping O'Sullivans from becoming a homogenous conveyor belt stud.

It had driven home to Iseult how lucky they were to have been bought out by Sheikh Nadim.

The Jeep came to a halt and Iseult got out, seeing that they were in another huge courtyard, with modern-looking stables on one side and a long, low one-storeyed building on the other. The building was L-shaped and crumbling, but she guessed in a deliberately artful way. It had the same stamp of Arabic design she'd noticed already. She also noticed the fact that it was cooler here than it had been in Al-Omar, which had to be due to the higher altitude.

A sound came from behind them, and she turned to see Sheikh Nadim greet the most stunningly beautiful woman Iseult had ever seen. She was dressed casually in jeans and a shirt, and her hair was a sleek fall of midnight-black down her back.

Her eyes were huge and piercingly blue—which, along with her olive skin, made Iseult think she had to come from somewhere almost mythical. She turned to face Iseult and a warm smile lit up her face, making her even more beautiful. She held out a hand. 'Hi, I'm Jamilah, the head groom. Welcome to Merkazad and the al Saqr stables.'

Iseult shook her hand and glanced up at Sheikh Nadim, who was frowning down at Jamilah. 'I thought I told you not to wait up.'

Something pierced Iseult deep inside when she

heard the obviously affectionate rebuke in his voice, and saw his concern. She looked back to Jamilah, who was still smiling. 'Of course I had to be up to meet Iseult—*and* this wonder horse you've been talking about. It was nothing. I just set my alarm for when I knew you'd be home.'

She walked around to where a stablehand had magically appeared to open the horsebox. Jamilah led Devil's Kiss out and gave him a thorough once-over, before saying with obvious appreciation, 'He really is a beauty. You've done a good job. I can see that you're going to be a welcome asset here, Iseult.'

Iseult blushed with pride. No one, apart from her father or grandfather, had ever complimented her before. And Sheikh Nadim had all but accused her of potentially ruining Devil's Kiss. 'Thank you.'

Iseult felt Sheikh Nadim's heavy gaze on her as she followed the stablehand who was now leading Devil's Kiss to his new home. It too was as luxurious as the horsebox had been.

She was trying desperately to ignore the fact that she felt so all over the place now that she'd noticed the special relationship between Jamilah and the Sheikh, and then Jamilah came alongside her and took her arm with friendly ease. She had Iseult's case in the other hand, and Iseult insisted on taking it from her.

'Come on—you must be exhausted after you've

been so summarily dragged across the globe. I'll show you to your rooms and you can rest. There will be plenty of time to show you around tomorrow.'

Iseult tried weakly to joke. 'I'd hardly call private air travel being dragged across the globe.'

Out of the corner of her eye she could see Sheikh Nadim raise his hand in a gesture to Jamilah, who nodded silently back to him. Easy communication flowed between them. He wasn't even making any attempt to say goodnight to *her*, and Iseult hated the fact that she'd noticed. Clearly he'd gone above and beyond the call of duty in meeting Iseult to bring her and Devil's Kiss here, and now couldn't wait to be gone. Perhaps he hadn't even trusted that she would have taken care of Devil's Kiss on the journey, and that was why he'd met them himself.

The Jeep and horsebox disappeared out of the stables area, and Jamilah led Iseult over to the long L-shaped building. She could see now, as they drew closer, that it must have been the old stables, now converted.

Jamilah had a key, and opened a door in the furthest part of the building and led Iseult in, turning on lights which sent out a low warm glow. Iseult came in and put down her suitcase. The downstairs was open-plan, with a kitchen and sitting area furnished in cool white and neutral tones. Up some stone stairs there was a comfortable and pristine bedroom and bathroom, again furnished in whites and creams. It screamed understated luxury, and was a million miles from the kind of accommodation staff would have been used to at O'Sullivan's stables, even in the good times.

Jamilah was explaining. 'They're all pretty much the same in this block. I'm in the one at the other end—nearest the stables. That's where my office is too. We have bigger ones for couples, and we have proper houses too, for staff with families, not far from here. I hope this is suitable for you?'

Iseult whirled around, aghast that Jamilah might have taken her stunned silence to mean anything else. 'It's wonderful. I had no idea what to expect, but it certainly wasn't anything as luxurious as this…'

Jamilah quirked a smile, and once again Iseult was struck by her beauty. 'Nadim takes care of his staff very well. That's one of the reasons why he's so respected and gets so much out of his workers.'

'You…' Iseult bit her lip. 'You call him Nadim… Don't we have to call him Sheikh?'

Jamilah laughed—a beautiful tinkling sound. '*No!* He'd hate that.' She slanted a stern look at Iseult, but her mischievous eyes told her not to take her too seriously. 'Nadim insists on informality, but that's not to say that everyone doesn't know their place and respects him as the ruler and supreme leader of Merkazad... Don't worry—you'll see how it works.' Jamilah led Iseult over to a low window and pointed outside. 'From here you have a view of the castle, that's where Nadim lives.'

Iseult looked out, and shivered when she took in the sight. The castle was more like a fortress—too huge and imposing to be described as beautiful. It was like the man himself. Effortlessly intimidating. It was built on a rocky outcrop which she guessed would have a view out over Merkazad and, like the other buildings she'd seen on their journey to the stables, Iseult recognised the Arabic influence. The wide sweeping archways and ornately intricate designs of the trellised stone perimeter glowed white in the moonlight.

'It dates from the sixteenth century, and although it's been updated and modernised on the inside, the outside is still the same as when it was a defensive castle. It has some of the best examples of intact Islamic murals on the Arabian peninsula. Scholars come from all over the world to study them.' Jamilah straightened up and smiled. 'I'll take you there and show you around in the next few days, when you've got your bearings.'

Iseult felt shy. 'Are *you* from here?'

A shadow seemed to pass across Jamilah's face just for an instant, and then she answered easily. 'Partly. My mother was from here, but my father was French. I was born in France, but then we came back here. My father worked for Nadim's father. My parents died in the same air crash that killed Nadim's parents, and as I had no other family he took me into his.'

'I'm sorry. I didn't mean to pry.'

Jamilah waved a hand. 'Don't be silly. It was all a long time ago. I owe Nadim everything.' She moved to go downstairs, and then turned back abruptly. 'And, despite what you may have thought just now, Nadim is like my older brother. Nothing more.'

Iseult blushed beetroot-red and stammered, 'I didn't…didn't think…anything like that…'

But Jamilah was already disappearing back downstairs, with an enigmatic smile on her face. Iseult followed her, mortified to think she'd been so obvious in her assessment of their relationship. If Jamilah had seen her reaction, had Nadim? Her insides curdled at the thought.

Jamilah showed Iseult a few more practical things about the accommodation, like where the food was stocked, and then left her, telling her that she'd come by to get her after she'd had a long lie-in in the morning.

That night, as Iseult lay in the strange bed, all she could think about was the fact that Nadim and the stunningly beautiful head groom weren't in a relationship. And her predominant feeling was one of something scarily like relief, when she had no earthly right or reason ever to imagine herself in any kind of a relationship with such a man.

CHAPTER FOUR

THE following morning Iseult was surprised to find that she'd slept right through, for about eleven hours. She could hear a hum of activity coming from outside, and after a quick shower and cup of coffee she went to investigate with something that felt suspiciously carefree in her chest. She'd never been in a situation where she wasn't automatically responsible for every little thing.

As soon as she opened her door she faltered on the doorstep. The sheer intense heat nearly knocked her sideways. She realised she'd have to go shopping at some stage. Her Irish wardrobe of long-sleeved T-shirts, jumpers and fleeces would be woefully too much for here.

There was an intense hive of activity before her. The quiet stables courtyard from last night had been transformed, and was now full of people all engaged in various activities. Iseult immediately felt guilty. At home she would have already been up for several hours and working.

Horses were being led to and from stalls—some by women in the long Muslim *abeyya*, with veils covering their hair. But others were in Western dress—jeans and T-shirts—which negated her suspicion that they had to dress in a more conservative fashion.

There were also a couple of Western staff. To her relief she could see Jamilah in the distance, waving to her from the stable where Devil's Kiss had been installed last night. Iseult walked over, smiling shyly at the people she passed, noticing one very friendly-looking blond man, who grinned at her appreciatively as he got out of a Jeep.

When she reached Jamilah the woman was sending a mock-censorious look to the young blond man. 'Stevie, shouldn't you be down at the equine pool this morning, to cover for Abbas?'

He saluted cheekily and sauntered off. Jamilah said, with a touch of weariness in her tone, 'Stevie Bourne is an incorrigible flirt, and already has a string of broken hearts all over Merkazad. If he wasn't such a good groom I'd have let him go a thousand times.'

After checking on Devil's Kiss, and seeing that he appeared to be getting over the journey well, Jamilah took Iseult off on a tour in a golf buggy.

She explained that it was the quickest way to get around the vast stables.

After just five minutes Iseult's mouth seemed to be welded open.

She'd seen some of the biggest stables and studs at home in Ireland, and they were impressive, but this—*this* was on another level altogether. At her own rough count she reckoned that she'd seen close to one hundred horses in training. Yearlings, colts, fillies and older. She'd spotted the magnificent Desert Rose, who had won at Longchamp the previous year, and who clearly, despite fevered media speculation, wasn't being retired to stud yet.

She was introduced to the head trainer, a quietly spoken Frenchman called Pierre, who had a select team underneath him. They had sand-based gallops, and also an extravagantly watered grass-based gallops too. Plus they had an impressive length of all-weather racetrack.

By the time Jamilah was heading back towards the main stables Iseult was feeling seriously overwhelmed, and felt even more so when she was led to a Jeep and told she was being taken to the stud, which was about two miles away. In the Jeep, Jamilah ascertained that Iseult didn't really have appropriate clothing for the heat, so they stopped off in Merkazad to get some clothes.

In the bright vibrancy of daylight Iseult could see that it was a bustling, heaving city. All the buildings were close together, and modern architecture nestled alongside ancient buildings teeming with history in a glorious mix. Women covered from head to toe, with beautiful flashing kohled eyes, passed her in the street, and dark men in *dishadashas*, with turbans on their heads.

Bedu nomads had set up in groups alongside the main road, erecting their tents into makeshift villages with beautiful dark-eyed children running back and forth.

Despite Iseult's protestations, Jamilah insisted that she would pay for the clothes, telling her she could put it against her first month's wages. Iseult had no choice but to accept.

The stud was as impressive as the stables, set in liberally watered and surprisingly lush grounds, with gorgeous stables to house all the stallions, mares and foals.

It was late afternoon by the time they got back to the main stables, and Iseult could see that Jamilah was anxious to get to her own work. She assured her she'd be fine now that she had an idea of where everything was, but had to quell the dart of loneliness when Jamilah disappeared.

After she'd checked on Devil's Kiss, and made herself something to eat, she found the communal common room that Jamilah had shown her earlier, where she could make a phone call to her father. To her intense relief he sounded fine, and even confided to Iseult, 'To be honest, love, this is the best solution. We could have lost everything. I know it's not ours any more, but our name is still on the gate and the new manager is a good man. I'm glad the stress of keeping the place going has been taken out of my hands…I'm looking forward to concentrating on training again.'

Iseult finally put the phone down after reminding her father that the twins were due home for a visit that weekend, to make sure that Murphy got his heart medication in his food, and that it was Mrs O'Brien's birthday tomorrow.

She nearly jumped three feet high when she heard a deep, drawling voice say from behind her, 'Still running operations from here?'

Her whole body exploded in a wave of heat as she turned slowly to face Sheikh Nadim. He was leaning nonchalantly against the wall near the door, dressed in a pristine dark suit and white shirt and tie. He looked so incongruously gorgeous against the plain background that she felt stunned, as if she might be imagining him. But when she blinked he didn't disappear.

Immediately Iseult felt self-conscious and stiff. 'I was just checking in—letting my father know that I'm safe and well.'

'And are you? Well?'

Iseult nodded, suspicious of Nadim's concern.

'Yes… Jamilah has been very kind, showing me around today.'

'You rested well last night?'

Iseult nodded again, her mouth twisted. 'The rooms are more than comfortable. I thought I'd be lucky to get the corner of a stable beside Devil's Kiss.'

Sheikh Nadim tutted and stood away from the wall. Immediately Iseult felt threatened. 'Such an imagination. All my staff are taken care of, Iseult. I don't believe in the outdated view that stable-hands are little better than skivvies.'

His obvious implication that that was all she was made Iseult's back straighten with innate pride. It was a long time since anyone had considered her just a stablehand. Her chin came up. 'You don't have to remind me of my place, Sheikh. I'm not exactly in a position to demand the right to keep training Devil's Kiss.'

When Iseult answered back, with that defiant little chin-tilt, Nadim had a split second of realising how inappropriate it had been to come here like this, on the pretext of seeing how she had settled in. He should have been content with the call he'd put in to Jamilah earlier, when he'd found that she was doing the grand tour with Iseult, even if at that moment Iseult had been in a changing room in a shop in town, trying on clothes. But when he'd driven through the main gate just a short while before he'd found himself instinctively turning towards the stables, unable to ignore the impulse to see her.

His jaw tightened and the self-recrimination running through him made his voice harsh. 'No, you don't have that right. We've yet to see you work. There are staff who've been here for a year and haven't earned the right to work under Pierre. And I won't have you dragging Jamilah off on shopping errands again. She's far too busy and valuable to the running of this place.'

The unfairness of his accusation made Iseult gasp. 'I didn't even want to go shopping. Jamilah saw that my clothes weren't suitable and kindly insisted on taking me, and I'm glad she did. Who knows when I might have got out? I'm well aware I'm just here on sufferance, because you have some idea that I'd do more damage than good back at home.'

Nadim fought the intense urge he had to stride over and haul Iseult against his too hot body, and quell her words in a very carnal way. He couldn't believe she was so effortlessly making his blood pressure zoom skywards within just minutes of seeing her again. He'd followed some rebel impulse to see her for himself and now *this*. There were plenty of foreign staff at his stables, and he'd never concerned himself about how *they* were settling in.

Sexual tension was so immediate and taut between them it could have been cut with a knife, and any hope Nadim might have had that bringing Iseult O'Sullivan here would diminish her effect on him was laughable. Despite being busy all day today, he hadn't been able to get her out of his mind.

In two quick strides he stood right in front of her, and saw how her eyes widened and a dark flush stained those alabaster cheeks. His hands were clenched into fists at his sides to stop himself from reaching out to loosen her hair and see it spread across her shoulders.

Wanting Iseult was completely inappropriate and unwelcome. He didn't sleep with staff, and she was a world away from the type of woman he would normally go for...

He gritted out, 'It's *Nadim*. No one here calls me Sheikh. And you are as free as anyone else to explore Merkazad on your days off. Jamilah has all the information you'll need on getting around.'

So abruptly that Iseult swayed on her feet Nadim turned and was gone again, taking his intense forcefield of energy with him and leaving a vacuum behind. Iseult sank down into a chair behind her. For a second there she'd had the overwhelming feeling that he was going to kiss her. Even now her mouth tingled in anticipation. She touched it lightly with her fingers and it felt sensitive to the touch. Her skin prickled all over, and down lower between her legs a pulse throbbed disconcertingly.

As abruptly as Nadim had left, Iseult stood and fled back to her rooms, shutting herself inside. Remembering the intensity of Nadim's eyes just now, she prayed that he wouldn't feel he had to check up on her again. Because evidently when he came within three feet of her she turned into someone else. Someone who couldn't control her tongue and who was reduced to a mass of heated desires.

To Iseult's intense disappointment her prayers were answered, and for the next two weeks she saw no sign of Nadim. She settled into a routine at the stables, and heard Jamilah say in conversation with others that Nadim was in Europe.

As much as that should have comforted her, it didn't. Despite everything, Iseult couldn't stop thinking about Nadim, and that hot intensity she'd felt between them the last time she'd seen him. Every minute of every day people referred to him in hushed, awed and reverent tones. But not one person had a bad word to say about him. And his knowledge and impeccable instinct when it came to horses was apparent all around her.

She wondered why it was that he was only just beginning to make a name for himself, when the stables and the stud had been in operation since his father's time. Jamilah had been uncharacteristically tight-lipped when Iseult had asked, and Iseult hadn't pursued it.

When Iseult had finished at the stables one day, after Nadim had been gone a fortnight, she walked over to the training grounds, where one of Pierre's assistants was supervising the exercising of Devil's Kiss. The assistant explained that Pierre had also gone to Europe for a few days.

One of the other trainers, a man called Alain, came over, looking seriously disgruntled. In the course of the conversation between the two men, it transpired that a yearling was proving difficult to break in.

Feeling curious, Iseult asked Alain, 'Can I have a look at him?'

The trainer shrugged nonchalantly. 'Be my guest. I was hoping to have good news for Pierre when he returned, and at least have the bit between his teeth, but it looks like only Nadim or Pierre will be able to tame this one.'

Iseult wandered over to a fenced-in area and saw the yearling. Her well-practised eye assessed him in an instant, and she felt a deep sense of satisfaction run through her. Also a deeply ingrained instinct. She could work with this yearling. She knew she could.

She took the bridle and bit off the fence, where

Alain had left them after his fruitless attempt. She was barely aware of the small crowd gathering as she climbed up and sat on the fence, just watching the horse for a long time. When she felt the time was right she slid down and into the enclosure, slowly starting to walk around, going in ever-decreasing circles closer and closer to the horse. She was unaware of the alarmed look passing between Alain and the other trainer.

She was unaware of anything but the horse. She always got like this when she was breaking in a horse. It was a silent communication that hummed between them, and she had no idea where it came from. She gently crooned words that her grandfather had used to use—old Gaelic words.

She was close enough to the horse now to touch him, and he stood still. Recognising her. With infinite gentleness and patience Iseult put the bridle over his head and the bit into his mouth. It was only when she realised the whispers had ceased that she looked up and became aware that everyone had scattered.

There was just one person standing there now: Nadim, with his face as dark as thunder, hands on lean hips.

Iseult's heart went out of control, as if she'd received a shot of adrenalin. She gulped guiltily, taking in the fact that he looked gorgeous after an absence of over two weeks. He was wearing jeans, and a T-shirt that moulded across his chest and showed off his taut musculature and broad shoulders.

Iseult took the bridle off the yearling again and patted him down, then walked back to the fence on shaky legs. The minute she had slipped out through the gate and closed it Nadim strode over and took her arm in a tight grip.

'Wait a second,' she protested. 'You're not even giving me a chance to—'

He silenced her with a thunderous look. 'Not a word. Jamilah's office *now*.' Nadim all but threw Iseult into his Jeep and drove the short distance to the main stables, tension crackling between them. Iseult was tight-lipped, with arms crossed.

When he drew to a halt Iseult jumped out and preceded him into Jamilah's office, aware of eyes everywhere taking this in. She knew very well that Nadim had a right to be angry with her for overstepping her mark—but *this* angry?

Jamilah was there too, but Nadim dismissed her with a curt instruction in guttural Arabic. She sent Iseult a questioning look as she walked out and quietly shut the door behind her.

Nadim raked a hand through his short hair and turned to face Iseult. She refused to be intimidated and waited for the explosion. But it didn't come. Nadim just said easily, 'Was it too much to expect that I might leave here for a couple of weeks and hope that you wouldn't get into trouble?'

But then she saw his flashing dark eyes, and the thin veneer of his civility became apparent. Iseult could sense that he was holding back with supreme control, and it made her quiver inwardly.

Even so, she hitched up her chin and crossed her arms defensively again. It was impossible for her not to react defensively with this man—he shook her right to her foundations. 'You're right. I shouldn't have gone into that enclosure. Why don't you just say what you've got to say and let me go?'

'Where did you get the nerve to think you could go near such a dangerous yearling and attempt something so foolhardy?'

Iseult saw a pulse throb in Nadim's temple and had to focus on his words. She frowned. *Dangerous?* What are you talking about? No one said anything about him being dangerous...' She was genuinely confused now.

'The reason that yearling is on his own and apart from the others is that no one has been able to get near him. I'd left explicit instructions that no one was to attempt anything with him until either myself or Pierre got back. Only three weeks ago he kicked one of the trainers, who luckily escaped with just a cracked rib.'

Iseult was stunned at this information—and

stunned to recognise how gullible she'd been. Clearly Alain and the other trainer had set the new girl up in spectacular style. 'I had no intention of doing anything in the first place. I was watching Devil's Kiss exercising and someone mentioned that they were having trouble with a yearling. I went to look at him, that was all.'

She stopped and looked away, and then back to Nadim. How could she explain this to him? 'But then, when I saw him, I just…saw that I might be able to handle him…and I did. I can't explain it. It's not something rational. If I'd had any idea he was considered so dangerous of course I wouldn't have gone in there. I'm not a complete idiot.'

Nadim folded his arms too, making Iseult feel hot in her belly when she saw his muscles bunch. Then he frowned suspiciously. 'No one encouraged you to try your hand at breaking him in?'

As much as Iseult knew that the trainers had been mischievous in deliberately misleading her, she wouldn't say anything. She'd walked into their trap. She was the newbie, and there under sufferance. She wouldn't do herself any favours by squealing.

So she shook her head miserably and said quietly, 'No.' And then more fiercely, looking directly at Nadim, 'It was purely my idea.'

Nadim dropped his arms and prowled close to Iseult, making her breath hitch. 'Apart from your arrogant boldness at thinking you could succeed where no one else had, no one in the training area is allowed to go in without adequate head protection, and that is non-negotiable. I've sacked trainers for not wearing proper protection.'

Iseult looked up at Nadim and dropped her arms. 'I was *not* being arrogant—I just saw the yearling and thought I might be able to help. And how would I know about wearing protection if no one thought to tell me?'

His blistering tone cut her off. 'Dammit, woman, do you have to argue with everything I say? You should be in the habit of wearing protective head gear no matter what. Horses are unpredictable. You had everyone mesmerised by your horse whisperer routine, so it's no wonder no one mentioned the hat. I promised your father I'd take care of you, but I can't do that if every time I turn my back you turn into a walking liability.'

To disguise the sharp pain which lanced her at the thought that his apparent concern was just born out of a sense of responsibility to her father, Iseult said cuttingly, 'Oh, so now you're best friends with my father, who you deemed unfit to run his own stud farm?'

In an instant Nadim had reached out to haul Iseult into his body, his hands tight around her upper arms. Iseult opened her mouth in shock, and had the split-second realisation that Nadim was going to kiss her just a breath before he did. She recognised in that moment that since she'd laid eyes on this man she'd wanted this, with a wild singing in her blood. There was not even a moment of hesitation. Every cell in her body was fizzing and jumping.

Iseult had never been kissed before. And certainly not like this. Not with such intensity that it felt as if she were burning up from the inside out. Somehow she was vaguely aware that Nadim had rested back against something and had pulled her even closer, right into the cradle of his thighs, where she could feel the shockingly hard press of his arousal. It made wet heat explode between her legs.

His hands finally let go of her arms to snake around her back, and of their own volition Iseult's hands went to the back of Nadim's head, tangling in the surprisingly silky strands of his hair. The moment went on and on, suspending them in time and space. It was as if Iseult's world had gone from zero to a thousand on a sensual voltage scale that she had no control over.

Iseult's mouth opened, instinctively seeking more, and Nadim groaned deep in his throat, his tongue meshing with hers in a hot dance. She could feel her hair being pulled free of her ponytail and falling in a heavy weight down her back. Nadim tugged on it gently, to force her head back, and she sucked in a gasp when she felt his mouth and lips trail hot kisses down her jaw and neck, finding where the pulse beat out of control and sucking there for a moment.

One hand snaked up under her T-shirt and Iseult's belly clenched in delicious anticipation when she felt him find and cup her breast. She groaned when she felt his impatience, and he snaked that hand around to open her tight sports bra, releasing her heavy breast into his hand.

With her eyes still shut tight, as if opening them might make the spell break, Iseult let Nadim guide her head back to him, and his mouth slanted hotly over hers again, tongue stabbing deep as that hand cupped and moulded her unfettered breast. Between his thumb and forefinger he caught the hard nipple and teased it, squeezing and pulling. Iseult's hands tightened around his skull—and in that moment she felt the shift in energy—as if they had both woken from the sensual spell at exactly the same time.

Iseult opened heavy-lidded eyes and looked into deep dark pools full of recrimination. She was breathing heavily, chest rising and falling, and Nadim still cupped her breast intimately.

With an abrupt move he put his hands on her arms again and physically moved her back. Iseult's legs felt so unsteady for a moment that she swayed and had to put out a hand to the back of a nearby chair.

Nadim's voice broke the taut silence. 'That shouldn't have happened.'

Iseult winced inwardly to hear Nadim say the words so curtly, and cursed herself. What had she expected—that he would take her in his arms and profess that he couldn't get her out of his head? That she was driving him mad with desire? And how had she gone from hating this man for taking a wrecking ball to her world less than three weeks ago to wanting him so badly right now that she shook all over?

'No, it shouldn't have happened,' she agreed faintly. She couldn't look up. Her shaking hands went behind her back to do up her bra, hiding her too voluptuous breasts from view once more. When she'd developed too early she'd got used to hiding her breasts, terrified that she'd get teased like other buxom girls at school. And then, with riding every day, it had been more practical to wear sports bras to contain them.

She saw his shoes come into her vision, and then a hand tipped her chin up. Even her skin there burned at his touch.

Nadim looked down into Iseult's eyes and had to hold back the wave of need spiralling through him again. It made a mockery of the trip he'd just taken to Europe in a bid to restore some sanity to his lust-hazed brain. It hadn't worked. Instead of forgetting about this witch he'd found himself waking in the night, aching all over with frustration. He hadn't stood a chance as soon as he'd seen her again. It galled him even more to acknowledge that he'd gone to such lengths to avoid her effect on him.

Iseult's mouth was swollen and pink and still moist. His body was taut, tight and aching with hot arousal. With unfulfilled need. But it had been a mistake to kiss her. Even if he had wanted Iseult on sight, and every moment between them had led to this explosion of lust, it couldn't happen again.

She was an employee. And a wayward, unpredictable one at that. He was the ruler of Merkazad and had a reputation to maintain. He was forgetting that far too often when he came within mere feet of this woman. But he was finding it hard to think right now, when she was so close. When her delicate natural scent wound around his body like a siren call. He had to resist her. She was not a sophisticate, and here at his stables it was too close to home, too close to raw memories.

He stepped back now, dropping his hand, but saw how Iseult's chin stayed defiantly hitched, even though her big amber eyes were still dark and wary, full of swirling emotions. Seeing that made something hard solidify in his chest, and made it easy for him to regain some perspective.

'It won't happen again.'

He raked a hand through his hair, leaving it dishevelled. 'Despite your behaviour today at the training ground, I'm prepared to let you move there under Pierre's tutelage once he's back in a couple of days. Perhaps if you're properly supervised in the area you seem to naturally gravitate towards, you'll be less of a liability.'

Before Iseult could reply Nadim had coolly walked out of the room. She sank back down into a chair behind her because her legs gave way. She heard muted tones outside and guessed that he was talking to Jamilah. A few minutes later there was silence, and then the sound of a Jeep starting up and driving away.

Jamilah came in, and Iseult couldn't look at her. She was too ashamed, and hated to think that perhaps Jamilah would suspect Nadim was moving her to work with Pierre because she'd manipulated him on purpose.

She looked up to see Jamilah making something like tea; when she sent her a quick look to ask if she wanted some, Iseult just shook her head. 'Jamilah, I—'

The other woman turned around, and Iseult quailed at the stern look on her face. Her belly fell.

'I know what Pierre's guys are like. As soon as he leaves Merkazad they turn into pranksters. I know they probably set you up—they've done it before.'

Iseult started to protest. 'But I never said anything to Nadim—'

'I know you didn't.' Jamilah was still grim, but then she smiled mischievously. 'When Nadim told me what had happened I put two and two together. To be honest I'd love to have seen their faces when you got into that enclosure and did what they couldn't do. It'll serve them right. They also probably got the fright of their lives when they realised you weren't wearing a hard hat...' Jamilah sat down on a chair near Iseult and said, more seriously now, 'I don't know if you've heard anything yet about Nadim's wife?'

Iseult's heart stopped dead. She could feel herself pale, and her hands gripped the chair. Nadim was *married*? And he'd just kissed her like *that*?

Jamilah seemed to read her mind and shook her head. 'He's not married any more. His wife died nearly four years ago now. Sara was killed when she took one of the colts out to ride; she wasn't a natural horsewoman. It threw her and kicked her in the head. She wasn't wearing protective head gear and suffered massive brain trauma. She was three months pregnant at the time. She and the baby died.'

Iseult went cold all over. 'That's horrendous.'

Jamilah continued. 'Nadim nearly closed the

whole stables and stud down…only in the past couple of years has he shown an interest again. That's why he went so berserk when he found you. He's obsessive about staff wearing head protection.'

Iseult bit her lip, something very dark gripping her at hearing the evidence of just how much he must have loved his wife. 'I had no idea.' She felt shaky all of a sudden. 'Has Nadim told you—?'

Jamilah quirked a brow. 'That he's moving you to Pierre? Yes. But anyone can see that training is where you should be. I told him that since you've been here you've put in more hours than anyone else, even though it's obvious how over-qualified you are…'

Iseult flushed, unaccustomed to being noticed for her work. She got up to go, protesting that Jamilah must have things to do. Jamilah stood too, and put a hand on Iseult's arm.

'I can see that there's something between you and Nadim.' Iseult blushed furiously, but Jamilah just continued gently, 'It was obvious from the moment he brought you here with Devil's Kiss himself.' She smiled a little wryly. 'And also while I was waiting outside just now there was an extremely long *silent* moment when you stopped shouting at each other. That's another thing—no one shouts at Nadim and gets away with it.'

Iseult blushed even harder.

Something tortured crossed Jamilah's beautiful face then, and she said, 'Just…be careful. The al Saqr men can be ruthless in their pursuit, and equally ruthless when they're finished with you. I'd hate to see you get hurt…'

Iseult frowned. 'What are you saying? Did you—?'

Jamilah shook her head. 'No, nothing has ever been between me and Nadim. I don't think about him like that. But his women didn't last long before Sara, and they don't last long now.'

Jamilah took a breath. 'He has a younger brother, Salman…' Her mouth twisted. 'Let's just say I've experienced their ruthlessness first-hand.'

Jamilah gave her a quick impetuous hug then, and Iseult felt tears prickle. She'd never had a close female friend before.

Feeling uncharacteristically emotional for the rest of the evening kept Iseult in her rooms. She sat by the window of her bedroom with her knees drawn up under her chin and looked at the harsh, imposing castle in the distance. She shivered. When Nadim had kissed her earlier she'd become something, *someone* else. Someone feminine and delicate. Sensual. And it was hard to acknowledge that part of herself. It was so alien.

That kiss had crystallised the feeling that had been born within her the very first moment she'd laid eyes on his image on the internet. It was the yearning of her long-buried femininity, wanting to unfurl like a flower and be allowed to breathe for the very first time.

Iseult grimaced. Well, not the very first time. She had explored what it was to be a desirable woman once before, but it had ended in such humiliation that she'd locked it away deep down inside, where she wouldn't have to look at it again.

That was why she found it so easy to brush off the effusive flirtations of someone like Stevie Bourne, the over-friendly groom she'd seen on her first day. She had a well-developed wall of protection around her. But Nadim… Iseult quivered deep inside. With Nadim she had no protection…

Thinking of this made the painful memory of her final year of school and the graduation dance surge back. As it had approached Iseult had fully expected not to be asked, as she'd always been too busy and too shy to flirt with the boys in her school. Losing her mum at a vulnerable age had made her feel awkward and self-conscious.

The other girls had long given up on asking her along to their weekly shopping trips, or including her in endless conversations full of gossip—not that Iseult had really minded; she'd had bigger concerns. But still…some of the girls had seemed to take it personally, and had jeered that she thought she was better than them. Iseult had learnt to ignore them, which she knew had probably made things worse.

But, to her absolute shock, as the dance had approached that last school year, the most handsome boy in the school had asked her out. She'd been too flattered and surprised to think logically about how unlikely it was, and hadn't been able to stop the flare of purely feminine excitement to think that perhaps life wasn't all about grief, work and responsibility.

The boy, Luke Gallagher, had told her he'd meet her in their local town's main square, under the clock, on the evening of the dance. Iseult's father had dropped her off, clearly delighted that his daughter was doing something for herself for a change.

With no spare money even then to splash out on a proper dress, Iseult had felt achingly self-conscious in an old dress of her mother's that she'd adjusted to fit her. She'd hoped that she'd achieved the 'vintage' look, but had an awful suspicion it just looked hideously out of date. When her little sister Nessa had told her she looked like a princess she hadn't had the heart to change.

Iseult had waited for a long time, with people walking past her and staring, before she'd had to face up to the fact that she was being spectacularly stood up. It would have been glaringly obvious what she was waiting for, as practically everyone knew everyone's business in the small town.

It had only been when it started to rain that she'd finally stood up from the seat and started to walk the long three miles home. At least in the rain she'd been able to give in to tears of embarrassment and rage, taking her high-heeled shoes off to walk barefoot when they became too painful.

Luke and some of the girls from school had passed her by in a flashy sports car then, blaring the horn, laughing and swigging from bottles of alcohol. But Iseult had just kept her head high and ignored them.

Even when Luke Gallagher had bumped into her a year later in the local supermarket, and made a blushing, stumbling apology—saying something about a stupid dare—it hadn't done much to assuage the deep hurt or her lingering mortification.

Iseult's focus came back into the room. Clearly Nadim had found her passably attractive for a brief moment, but it was crystal-clear that he'd regretted kissing her almost as soon as he had. The fact that he didn't relish seducing an employee had been etched all over his face, and had made her feel cheap and grubby.

That treacherous yearning to be found desirable and feminine would just have to be pushed back down to where it belonged. She couldn't bear to be hurt like that again, so no way was she going to let Nadim know how he effortlessly connected with such a secret part of her.

CHAPTER FIVE

NADIM sat back in his chair in the informal dining area of his private suite at the castle. He held a glass of whisky in his hand and swirled the dark amber liquid around, but his body tightened with predictable inevitability when the colour of the liquid reminded him of Iseult's eyes, and the way she'd looked at him after he'd kissed her to within an inch of their lives.

Disgusted anew at his woeful lack of control, he swallowed back the liquid in one gulp, relishing the burn down his throat as if it could burn away the desire that still hummed through his body. Something caught his eye then, and familiar guilt gripped him like a vice when he saw the sweet face of his dead wife smiling out benignly from a photo on the table nearby.

The pervading lingering guilt he felt at having been responsible for not only her death but their unborn child's had prevented him from putting away reminders like photos. It was like an open wound—guilt mixed in with ineffectual anger. And it served as a reminder never to let another woman get close enough to be hurt by him again.

In a reflex move Nadim surged to his feet and put the photo face-down. His hand was shaking. He'd never done that before. But then he'd never had to deal with such desire on his doorstep before... he'd always made sure to keep his affairs discreet and far away from Merkazad. Which was why this growing obsession with Iseult was so unwelcome. She was a world apart from the women he took as lovers now, and every instinct told him that she could be exactly the type to get hurt...

Nadim's hand tightened around the glass as he recalled the sheer panic that had gripped him when he'd seen her in that enclosure with the wild yearling, as blasé as anything.

He'd seen red. He'd actually thought he might be ready to send Iseult home. Anything had to be better than having her torturous presence there, under his feet. But instead of telling her to pack her things he'd hauled her into his arms and kissed her, any resolve not to get involved dissolving in a wave of lust so strong he hadn't been able to fight it.

Just then his chief aide Hisham came into the room and bowed. 'Sir, the conference call you requested has been set up in your private office.'

Nadim turned. 'Thank you.' As he strode out

behind Hisham it struck him as faintly ridiculous that he was allowing someone as unsophisticated as Iseult to get under his skin so easily.

Clearly he needed a new mistress, that was all. And when he went to B'harani in two weeks' time for the Sultan's birthday party he'd find someone eminently suitable there. Polished, mature, acqui-escent, invulnerable...*not* someone who dressed like an eighteen-year-old boy, wore too-tight sports bras to hide her breasts, and yet had the temerity to talk back to him and kiss him like no woman had ever kissed him before.

Two days later Iseult was still feeling skittish, jumping two feet in the air whenever anyone looked sideways at her. She'd seen Nadim from a distance earlier that day, for the first time in the traditional Merkazadi dress. In theory he should have looked ridiculous in the long flowing cream robes, with the distinctive turban on his head, but it had made an ache of gigantic proportions settle low in her belly. He'd looked even more exotic and regal, showing some guests around the stables. Iseult had had to use every ounce of her ability to stay focused on the job and listen to what Pierre was saying.

She was walking Devil's Kiss back to his stables later that evening and that ache was still in her belly, even though she hadn't seen Nadim in hours.

She felt wrung out. A curious tension was in the air, and she was glad to find the stableyard empty, all the other horses having been returned to their stalls. After hosing Devil's Kiss down with cool water, and making sure he was settled, she turned around to leave and nearly jumped out of her skin to see Stevie Bourne lounging against the stable door, watching her.

Iseult felt a little annoyed. Stevie had been becoming more and more persistent in the last few days. 'Stevie, you scared me half to death.'

Stevie came in and closed the stable door behind him.

Immediately Iseult felt threatened. 'I was just leaving. What are you doing here?'

He came closer, his blue eyes glinting. Iseult knew that plenty of the other girls fancied him, but he held no appeal for her. She tried to step around him now. 'Stevie, look, I'm tired and I need to get some dinner—'

With surprising speed he blocked her, so that now Iseult was trapped between him and Devil's Kiss. She knew that Devil's Kiss could get antagonistic in small spaces, with too many people around him. He was already moving impatiently, as if he'd had enough of these humans taking up his space.

Stevie backed Iseult into the corner and put an arm on either side of her head, trapping her. Iseult didn't feel threatened any more, she just felt exasperated. 'Stevie, stop it. I don't feel that way about you.'

He just smiled his most seductive smile, and Iseult felt faintly ill. 'Come on, Iseult, you don't know what you're missing. And I've missed you around here. It's not fair you got moved over to Pierre so quickly. There's a rumour, you know, that Nadim favours you.'

Iseult blushed and put up her hands to try and push Stevie away. 'That's ridiculous. Now, please *move back*.'

'Not until you kiss me.'

Iseult could feel Devil's Kiss move more impatiently now, and sensed that a kick could be coming their way any minute. But Stevie was immovable, and his strength sent a dart of panic through her as she blurted out, 'I'm not going to kiss you. Now, *move*.'

She leant forward, aiming to push him out of the way, but in a lightning-quick move he pulled her into him, pinioning her arms to her sides, and kissed her furiously, with little finesse.

Iseult couldn't breathe, and started to panic in earnest while still being very aware of Devil's Kiss beside them.

Suddenly through the wave of rising panic Iseult heard an arctic, 'What the *hell* is going on in here?'

Stevie moved back so abruptly that Iseult stumbled against the back wall. She automatically wiped the back of her hand across her mouth. Nadim stood in the doorway of the stable, holding onto Devil's Kiss's head. He filled the doorway with his huge frame, and Iseult saw the rope belt around his waist, an ornately decorated curved dagger thrust into it. In her eyes at that moment he could have been an ancient warrior king.

She couldn't take her eyes off him.

Stevie blustered, 'Iseult called me in here. I thought she needed a hand with Devil's Kiss, but—'

Nadim cut him off ruthlessly. 'Get out of here *now*, Bourne. And don't let me see you at the stables for at least a week.'

Stevie scarpered like the coward he was, and Iseult stood shakily, aware that Devil's Kiss had calmed right down now that Nadim was here. She walked forward on jelly legs.

Before she could even get a word out Nadim said fatalistically, 'That's it. This time you've gone too far.'

Iseult's inner fire rose, even though she felt wobbly all over. 'I am *not* going to take the blame for that. Stevie is a pathological flirt and *he* followed *me* in here. He wouldn't leave when I asked him—'

Nadim folded his arms. 'So you thought you'd

persuade him by kissing him? Give me a break. I know what I saw.'

'No, you don't. I did *not* welcome that kiss.'

Nadim arched a brow. Sarcasm dripped from his tone. 'You didn't welcome it in the same way that you didn't welcome my kiss the other day?'

Iseult's face flamed. She looked down at the ground and mumbled, 'That was different.'

Nadim had moved into the stable, and the air seemed to contract around them. Iseult looked up warily and was aware that this was totally different from how it had been with Stevie. Devil's Kiss, the traitor, now stood as still as a placid statue.

'*How* different?'

Iseult looked up into Nadim's dark eyes, in awe of him dressed like this, and said huskily, 'Because I liked being kissed by you…'

Iseult couldn't even feel chagrined at her honesty. She simply couldn't lie when Nadim stood before her like this. All her good intentions, her very necessary intentions of protecting herself around this man, were dissolving like wispy ineffectual clouds. That deep secret inner part of her was unfurling like a bud in the sun. She tried desperately to cling onto how disposable she'd felt after he'd kissed her the other day, but she was fast losing any grip on reality.

Nadim came even closer and snaked out a hand. His thumb came to her lips and rubbed back and forth, and his eyes got even darker. Iseult pulsed deep inside in response. The air was thick and heavy around them.

Nadim spoke roughly, his eyes fixed on her mouth. 'I don't like the thought of another man's taste on your lips.'

Iseult tried to shake her head but it felt heavy. His thumb still rubbed her lips. 'Neither do I.'

Obeying some primal urge from deep within her, Iseult stepped right up to Nadim and went on tiptoe, reaching to pull his head down. Her heart kicked and a light sweat broke out all across her skin when with a muffled groan Nadim's head came down and his mouth covered hers with barely restrained violence.

Mouths opened on a breath, tongues tangling intimately, hotly. It felt as if Nadim was branding her, eradicating any evidence of the other man, and Iseult welcomed it.

Nadim's hands moved down her back to cup her bottom, pulling her up and into him, where she could feel the hard evidence of his arousal through the voluminous robe. Iseult's hips moved in a silent and eloquently feminine plea against him, her hands smoothing across his shoulders, revelling in their broad strength.

Nadim tore his head away and looked down at Iseult's face, at her flushed cheeks and her mouth that looked beestung with arousal. She hadn't looked like this after Stevie had kissed her just now, and Nadim felt an intense surge of masculine satisfaction run through him. Quick on its heels came anger, swift and bright, at the acknowledgement that blind rage had nearly had him ripping Stevie Bourne limb from limb.

She'd done it again. Reeled him in like a fish on a line. He put his hands on her shoulders and put her back from him. She opened her eyes with an effort. She looked stunned.

Once again Nadim's lack of control seared him inwardly. He watched as Iseult tried to compose herself, and even now, though he knew it was sheer madness, he just wanted to shut the door and throw her down onto the hay, where he could sate himself properly.

He followed an instinct too strong to ignore, not even thinking of the ramifications of his decision. His voice was grim. 'I want you to go back to your rooms right now and pack your things.'

CHAPTER SIX

ISEULT felt as if she'd just been punched in the gut. Ice trickled through her veins. 'You're sending me home?'

Nadim was grim, his features stark. 'The next best thing.'

Iseult struggled to comprehend. She still felt spaced out—dizzy. 'What do you mean…? Where are you sending me?'

'You're moving up to the castle. You've proved that I can't trust you to stay out of trouble. Perhaps you'll stay out of trouble if you've got less time to tempt the staff down here.'

Nadim turned as if to go, and Iseult reached out on a reflex to grab Nadim's robe. 'Now, wait just a minute.'

Slowly Nadim turned around to face Iseult again, but she refused to let him intimidate her. She kept a tight hold on the sleeve of his robe. 'Why should I be the one to be punished when Stevie came after me?'

Nadim arched a brow. 'And within mere minutes of kissing him you were throwing yourself at me?' His mouth twisted faintly. 'You've proved that your taste is not only indiscriminate but insatiable.'

The words *But you kissed me back* died on Iseult's lips. She blanched to recall how she had stepped up to Nadim and pulled his head down, how she had pretty much begged him to kiss her. She let go of his robe. Self-doubt assailed her. *Had* he really kissed her back, as she'd believed he had? With the same level of passion? Or had it all been a figment of her twisted imagination? Had that awful yearning to be desired fabricated his response? The knowledge shamed her now.

She looked at Nadim steadily. He would *not* see what he was doing to her. 'If I move up to the castle what will people think?'

Nadim's jaw clenched. 'That is not for you to worry about.'

'But I will be working here. I have to face these people every day.'

Nadim came close to Iseult again, and as predictably as the sun rising in the morning she could feel her resolve dissolving again.

'No one questions what I do, or the decisions I make. I am the Sheikh, and that is something you would do well to remember. Leaving you here to your own devices is not something I'm prepared to do any more. Every day you will report for work as usual, and every evening you will return to the castle and your rooms there.'

'So I'm to be a virtual prisoner?'

Nadim quirked a mocking smile. 'Oh, I don't think you'll feel like a prisoner when you see your new rooms, Iseult. And you're free to leave at any moment. No one is stopping you.'

Iseult ignored the dart of alarm at the thought of that, and retorted caustically, 'No—only the fact that if I do leave I risk jeopardising my entire family's future...'

He moved to the door and said coolly, 'I'll let Jamilah know, and she can bring you up once you've packed your things.'

Iseult stood in the imposing main courtyard of the castle, completely intimidated. The very stones beneath her feet oozed history. Holding onto her one suitcase, she felt as if she'd just travelled a thousand miles into some Arabian fantasy—not just up the long drive from the stables with Jamilah in a Jeep.

The walls were so high she couldn't see anything beyond them, and carved into the huge slabs of stones were Arabic letters, swirling and graceful. The place was reverent, hushed.

Jamilah came around the front of the Jeep. Taking Iseult by the arm, she led her into the castle.

As soon as they walked through the giant looming archway light exploded around Iseult and she realised they were in another courtyard, but smaller, with a warren of pathways snaking off in every direction. Huge tall columns extended down these paths as far as the eye could see. As opposed to the almost austere main courtyard this one was full of small trees and plants. A pond with a small burbling waterfall graced the centre and even as Iseult watched a small iridescent fish leapt high and then fell back into the water.

Jamilah drew her attention to a small figure hurrying towards them, covered from head to toe in the traditional *abeyya* and *burka*, with just the most beautiful and enormous dark eyes visible.

Her belly was twisted in knots as Jamilah introduced the girl to Iseult. 'This is Lina. She'll be your personal maid while you're here, and show you to your rooms.' Iseult turned and gaped at Jamilah, who just smiled wryly. 'You're in another world now, Iseult.'

Iseult couldn't speak, and just watched helplessly as Jamilah looked at her watch and grimaced. 'I'd love to stay and help you settle in, but we've got a horse arriving any minute now. I'd better get back…' She gave Iseult a quick hug and said, 'You'll be fine. I'll see you tomorrow…' And then she was gone, her slim figure walking away quickly.

Still stunned at the evidence of the sheer grandeur around her, Iseult followed Lina down a dizzying maze of pathways and corridors. Some were covered and some were not, with the darkening dusky sky visible and lending an even more magical quality to the whole place.

Even though the castle was stunning, breathtaking, there was an air of a mausoleum about it. There should be the sounds of children running about, more hustle and bustle. Iseult's heart clenched when that made her think of what Jamilah had told her about Nadim's wife and baby. If his wife hadn't died presumably he'd have a small family by now.

They passed through a door in an ornately latticed wall and Lina came to a stop outside another door, halting Iseult's dangerously wandering thoughts. She opened it and gestured for Iseult to enter. Iseult walked in, her heart thumping, to see a room of such understated luxury that she simply couldn't believe it. Thick carpets felt like clouds of air. Everything was cream and dark gold. The sitting room they'd entered led into a bedroom the size of the dining room at Iseult's house at home, with a bed the size of her entire bedroom dominating the space.

The bathroom was pure opulence, with a sunken bath and an enormous shower. Open terrace doors led from the bedroom to yet another courtyard, and when Iseult stepped out she could see that it was bursting with a wild profusion of flowers. The scent was more heady than any perfume she'd ever smelt.

She turned back to see Lina watching her.

'There must be some mistake… This can't possibly be my room…'

The girl shook her head and took Iseult's case firmly out of her hand. She said in softly accented English, 'This is where you are to sleep. You are in the women's quarters. This is your room.'

Lina was opening the case and sorting through Iseult's clothes, and Iseult put out a hand, mortified to see this luxurious room tainted by her rags. 'No, please—you don't have to do that.'

But Lina ignored her and kept unpacking. A knock sounded on the main door, and Iseult went out to see another similarly clad girl entering with a silver tray covered in small plates and bowls of food. The smells were mouthwatering. Before Iseult knew it she'd been manoeuvred to the sitting room, where she was shown to a dining area. A low table was on the ground, and the girl was putting out the food, indicating that Iseult should sit down, cross-legged, on one of the huge silk cushions.

Another set of open doors led out to the courtyard from here, and, thoroughly bemused, Iseult could only sit and watch speechlessly as Lina and the other girl took their leave through them. Lina stopped at the door and said, 'I'll come back in an hour to run your bath.'

Iseult jumped up. This was going too far. *'No!'* She saw the way the other girl seemed to flinch slightly and moderated her tone. 'Sorry, I didn't mean it like that. All I mean is that there's really no need. I can manage on my own.' She gestured to the food. 'And thank you for this…but in future can't I just go to the kitchen or something?'

Lina seemed to giggle, and held a hand up to her mouth. She shook her head. 'No, Miss Iseult. This is how it is here. You are a guest of the Sheikh. I've been instructed to wake you at six in the morning…if you're sure you won't require any further assistance?'

Iseult shook her head quickly and the girl left. The reminder of her wake-up call brought her back to earth a bit. She might be living in these spectacular rooms now, but tomorrow she'd be back at the stables and working hard, and she had no doubt at all that Nadim wouldn't be paying her another visit.

She wondered where his rooms were within the vast castle, and then chastised herself, sitting down again to eat some of the deliciously prepared food. She tried to focus instead on what she'd been doing that day with Pierre, but every second moment the sheer opulence of her surroundings would floor her again, and all her mind could do was helplessly gravitate to the tall dark man who was turning her upside down and inside out.

Nadim heard nothing. He knocked again. Still nothing. Dammit—where was she? With a surge of something hot within him that he labelled anger, and not something more sexually primal, Nadim opened Iseult's door and went in. Silence greeted him, and he saw the remnants of her dinner on the low table in the sitting room.

With the carpet muffling his steps he walked into the vast bedroom—and stopped dead at the sight before him. One light threw out a halo of a dim glow. Iseult lay asleep on the bed, with just a short white towel wrapped around her body. One arm was flung up by her head, in a curiously child-ish gesture, the other across her belly. Her hair had been wrapped in another towel turban-style, but it had come loose and now a long skein of damp hair rippled across the pillow beside her, a stain of red against the pristine white cotton. Her skin was almost as pale as the sheets she °lay on.

For a second sheer lust threatened to blind Nadim as his gaze dropped and he took in the swells of her breasts against the towel. And her endless legs. Her thigh muscles were toned and strong from years of riding, and all he could imagine now was how they might feel clamped around his waist as he drove into her welcoming heat again and again. How she would arch her back so that he could feel her breasts crushed against his chest.

In an effort to claw back his rapidly disappearing control Nadim looked around the room. Her jeans were hung tidily on the back of an ornately brocaded chair, with what looked like a fresh shirt and clean underwear. This evidence of her setting out her clothes so methodically for the next day made something in his chest feel weak.

He should be walking away, retracing his steps back out of her room. He should never have come here, and he should not come here again. He should not be wanting her this badly, with a raging fever in his blood. He should not have moved her here, to the castle. He should never have brought her here from Ireland.

And yet as his treacherous gaze settled once again on the woman on the bed he knew he would fight off an army if they came to take her away from here, from him. There was also that very unwelcome sense of protectiveness he'd had ever since he'd realised the size of the burden she'd been carrying for years in maintaining the O'Sullivan stud. Even now he could see that those purple shadows that had been under her eyes had faded away, and the angular thinness he'd first noticed was softening.

In that moment Iseult's long-lashed eyes fluttered

open, and the breath left Nadim's body when he saw their dark amber glow settle on him.

Iseult lay very still on the bed. Was she awake or was she dreaming? She was lying on the softest bed she'd ever known, and in the dim seductive light Nadim was just standing there, watching her, dressed in a snowy white shirt and dark trousers, his beautiful harsh face set into shadows by the light. His tall lean body looked intimidatingly powerful and awe-inspiring.

She blinked, and as if a spell was broken Nadim took a step back and turned, walking swiftly out of her room. She heard the faintest click of the main door closing.

Reaction set in; her heart hammered painfully and she felt the most curious wrenching feeling. Her whole body tingled, as if Nadim had walked over to her and twitched the towel aside to look at her. The image was so audacious that Iseult had to question very seriously if she'd just experienced a hallucination.

To wake like that and see him there…it couldn't be possible. The fact that no words had been spoken seemed to make it even more dreamlike. Iseult sat up and felt seriously disorientated. The heavy damp length of her hair fell down her back. And yet all she could think of was how the persistent ache within her gnawed with renewed intensity…and all because her traitorous mind was now conjuring up three-dimensional apparitions.

She stood from the bed, and wobbled a little precariously before striding purposefully to the bathroom to dry her hair. This was ridiculous. She was twenty-three, she'd never been kissed properly until Nadim had kissed her for the first time, and she was a virgin. She was also hurtling headlong into a crush of monumental proportions on a man so out of her league at every possible level that it was ludicrous.

She winced as she ran the brush through her hair before drying it, and ignored the too-bright glitter of her eyes in the mirror. From now on she was here to work, and not to dream or moon or have hallucinations. *Work*—that would be her salvation, and in time she would request that she be sent home so that a few oceans and thousands of miles would be put between her and this dark nemesis of her vulnerable imaginings.

After a broken night of sleep, gritty-eyed, Iseult heaved a deep sigh when she saw delicate lines of pink usher in the dawn in the sky outside. Just then she heard the sound of a solitary voice calling people to prayer. She'd grown used to it since she'd arrived, coming at regular points in the day, but here in the castle it was much clearer.

Obeying an instinct to follow the sound, Iseult

got out of bed and pulled on a short silk robe over her T-shirt and knickers, and on bare feet went out of her bedroom. Everything was still and hushed, and the slightly cool morning air made goose-bumps pop up on her skin.

Still half asleep, she wandered down the long corridor, following the sound of the chant which was getting louder and clearer. She passed ornately decorated doors and other corridors which led down to mysterious passages, and then one in particular caught her eye. She investigated, and spotted old stone steps leading up to a higher level.

Climbing up, she went through a tiny door and emerged outside with a little gasp of delighted surprise. She could see that she was on one of the castle's open rooftop terraces, with a stunning view over Merkazad. She went over and stood by the wall, letting her hands rest on it.

Lights were winking off as the sun rose, and the small city glowed pearlescent against the blush stained sky. The distinctive minarets of the main mosque pierced the skyline, and that evocative and melodic chant against the stark silence of the morning made something deep within Iseult tug in a very primal way.

'It's the Muezzin, issuing the *adhan*.'

Iseult whirled around so fast she felt dizzy, and even dizzier to see Nadim leaning nonchalantly against a wall behind her in faded jeans and a crumpled T-shirt, as if he too had just stumbled out of bed and thrown them on. Dark stubble shadowed his jaw, making it look even harder. He looked as if he hadn't slept either, and liquid heat invaded Iseult's veins.

'I…didn't think anyone would be up.'

Hands in pockets, Nadim hitched his chin towards the city and pushed off from the wall to come and stand closer to Iseult. She couldn't take her eyes off him. He looked like a devilish angel, not the supreme ruler of a country. 'The whole city will be stirring now, and getting up to face another day.'

He wasn't looking at her, just facing out to the city, and Iseult followed his gaze, suddenly feeling very undressed and very vulnerable as she remembered last night. She longed to blurt it out—*Were you in my room last night or was I dreaming?*—but right now she felt certain that it had to have been a dream, a treacherous fantasy.

'Why did you come up here?'

Nadim's voice sounded harsh, and she sensed he was angry with her for disturbing his peace. Iseult could feel his eyes rake over her, and one of her hands gripped the robe tight at her breasts. Imposing a huge strength of will, she avoided looking at him, certain that his proximity would show him how affected she was by him.

Her voice was unbearably husky. 'I heard the

chant and…I don't know…it seemed to call to me. It's beautiful.'

'Yes, it is.' Nadim's voice had softened perceptibly. 'And it *is* a call. It's meant to make you want to follow it, to express your devotion.'

Unable not to, Iseult snuck a glance up at Nadim, and the breath stalled in her throat when his dark gaze caught hers. He was looking at her so intently. She felt as if *he* was issuing some silent call, because right now if he'd taken her hand and asked her to follow him anywhere she would have said yes.

Iseult was in serious danger of drowning in those dark dark eyes, but from deep within her some self-preserving instinct kicked in: the memory of how he'd kissed her came back, and the obvious self-recrimination he'd shown. *Both times.* She heard herself saying, 'You must miss your wife…'

Immediately there was a reaction. Nadim's jaw tightened and those eyes flashed. But her question had had the desired effect; in that mere second she could feel the distance yawn between them, even though physically he hadn't moved an inch. And, conversely, Iseult regretted saying anything.

'I shouldn't be surprised you've heard.'

'I'm sorry… I can't imagine what it must have been like to lose her.'

'You're forgetting it wasn't just her…it was our

baby too.' Nadim's face was tight with anger, his voice as harsh as she'd ever heard it.

Now Iseult felt about as low as it was possible to feel. Why on earth had she opened her big mouth? She flushed and moved back. 'I'm sorry, Nadim, I didn't mean…I didn't want to make you think of this…'

He laughed, and it sounded bitter. 'Don't worry. I don't need you to remind me of something that's seared into my brain.'

Finally he looked away for a moment, and Iseult felt the breath whoosh through her as if he'd held her suspended. Her heart squeezed at the bleak look crossing his face, even as a pain seemed to pierce right through it at the same time.

The assertion reverberating in her head tumbled out. 'You must have loved her a great deal.'

He slanted a look down at her, his face closed and stark. But then his mouth turned up in a cynical smile, and it sent a shot of trepidation through Iseult.

'That's just the thing. I didn't love my wife. It was an arranged marriage. But she loved me… she expected more from me than I could give.' He smiled mockingly, obviously seeing something on her face that she wasn't even aware of. 'Does that shock you, Iseult? Do you think we're barbarians here for arranging marriages like that? For not falling in love only to divorce two years later, like the Western world?'

Iseult shook her head. Her brain throbbed. He sounded so *hard*, and in that moment she felt a surge of sympathy for his wife having entered such a cold marriage. To have loved this cold, implacable man.

Nadim's mouth was a grim line now. 'This is normal here, Iseult. I am the Sheikh. I above anyone else am expected to make a good match, a practical match. It's not about falling in love.' He nearly sneered when he said those words. 'People get married every day, and it's for many reasons. Love rarely, if ever enters into it. To expect love is to expect too much.'

'But your wife did… Perhaps she just couldn't help herself.' Iseult had intended it to come out with a sarcastic edge, but she just sounded sad.

Nadim's eyes bored down into hers, and bitterness rang in his voice. 'She should have known better. Like I said, she expected too much. And don't think a day goes by when I'm not aware of what I couldn't give her—what I can't give any woman.'

It was almost as if he'd resigned himself to some kind of fate, and that bleakness reached out and touched Iseult like a cold hand. She shivered, and saw Nadim's eyes drop and take in her bare legs.

When his eyes rose again her body temperature had risen with them.

Had he moved closer? Iseult felt as if he had, even though the same space was still between them. He didn't move to touch her, but in that moment their eyes locked. Iseult felt as if Nadim was making some decision, staking some silent claim. As if he'd sent her some telepathic communication to say the subject of his wife was closed and the focus was back on her.

Something almost tangibly primal moved between them, and Iseult would have to have been made of ice not to notice it. The skin all over her body tingled, and she felt in great danger even as a treacherous lick of excitement kicked through her. She told herself fiercely that it had to be just her rampant imaginings—*had to be.*

The Muezzin's last chant was fading away on the morning air. And Nadim just said, 'Shouldn't you be getting ready for work?'

Iseult's hand still gripped her robe, and with a strangled reply of something inarticulate she forced her legs to move and fled. Nadim hadn't even touched her, but as she half stumbled back down the stairs and to her room she felt as though she'd been branded in some way…and, worse, as if she'd given him some tacit signal of acquiescence.

* * *

'I think you should take Iseult with you to the horse festival this weekend.'

Nadim looked at Pierre and bit back the urge to flatly refuse the suggestion, trying to block out the image of how she'd looked that morning, when she'd appeared like an apparition in front of him on the terrace.

'Why do you think that?'

The older Frenchman looked at Nadim. 'I've never seen anything like her talent, Nadim. She's truly extraordinary—light years ahead of some of the guys I've had working with me for years. I will admit that her technique is a little rudimentary and rough around the edges, but that's only from being largely self-taught. She told me her grandfather was her biggest influence, and I remember him well. He too had the same gift that put him above and beyond other trainers. Unfortunately he died when she was young, so she missed out on a lot of his teaching. But she has an expert eye—I think she could be very valuable to you if you see any pure-breeds in the mix up there.'

Pierre was referring to the annual Bedouin horse fair—the biggest gathering of native Arabian horses in Merkazad and Al-Omar each year. It was held high on a plateau in the northern mountains that bordered the two countries, and comprised buying and selling horses, and races and other social events.

It was also a chance for him to get out to the further reaches of his country and see his people.

Nadim made a non-committal response and welcomed the interruption of one of Pierre's staff asking a question. He was still reeling from his encounter with Iseult that morning. And still reeling from the fact that she'd managed to somehow get him to reveal far more than he ever would have intended about his wife and his marriage. Not many knew the bald facts, and he had to concede now that, despite coming from a culture of arranged marriages, most of his people would have harboured the fantasy that he had loved his wife.

Iseult had caught him off guard. *How* had she known to come to the one place in the whole castle that was his private space? When he was much younger he used to go up there and look out onto the view, contemplating the terrifying fact of his fate and the prospect of one day taking responsibility for an entire country.

No one had ever disturbed him there. It had been the one place he could escape from his brother, parents, obligations…his wife and the love he couldn't return, the awful guilt of that… But now something, *someone*, had superseded all of that.

He'd gone back to his room last night and hadn't been able to sleep a wink, with frustration coursing through his body. Eventually he'd gone out there to try and clear his head, get some perspective…

and then *she'd* appeared in front of him like a taunt, in that flimsy half-robe, long legs bare, hair in a tousled tangle down her back. The seductive shape of her body had been more than clear, her face fresh and clear of any make-up, and those eyes— He cursed as his body tightened with annoying predictability.

As he'd looked in her eyes that morning a sense of inevitability had washed through him. He either sent Iseult home and forgot about her, moved on with a new mistress, or else he slaked this desire and got her out of his system once and for all. And he already knew what his only choice was...

CHAPTER SEVEN

THE following day Iseult was sitting in the back seat of one of the Jeeps which was following Nadim out of Merkazad and up into the mountains. Two of his bodyguards sat in front, and a veritable retinue of vehicles snaked behind them, including a couple of empty horseboxes. Nadim was in the vehicle just ahead of them, and he'd barely glanced at Iseult before they'd set off from the main courtyard of the castle. He'd been dressed in traditional dress again—a long cream *thobe*, with a gold-trimmed robe over it.

She was still getting her head around the fact that Nadim had asked her to accompany him on this trip. Iseult had been in too much shock early that morning as in her half-sleep she'd let Lina chatter and manoeuvre her around and pack her a bag. And then before she'd had time to draw breath they'd been getting into the vehicles and were on their way. She had no idea why Nadim would want her to go along on such an expedition.

They were driving through the rockiest terrain Iseult had ever seen. Every now and then she caught a tantalising flash of abundant green and colour, and was reminded of when Nadim had told her that they'd just had a monsoon. It was hard to believe, driving through such an inherently arid land.

They drove ever upwards, and finally came to a halt. One of the bodyguards stepped out and opened Iseult's door, and when she got out into the bright sunlight and searing heat she could see Nadim waiting just a few feet away. He was looking at her, but then looked away.

Instantly her body reacted with a disturbing rush of desire. She stiffened her shoulders and walked over to him, seeing that some of the vehicles had kept going and the rest of the convoy had stopped in a kind of lay-by.

Hesitant, she stood beside him and followed his gaze, gasping when she did so. The whole of Merkazad was laid out before them from this vantage point. She could see the city shimmer in the far distance, and way beyond that the craggy crests of more mountains. Amidst the aridity were huge pockets of oases, in green and colours so beautiful that Iseult wanted to rub her eyes. In the near distance a magnificent waterfall cascaded down a mountainside.

It was like a vision of that mythical place

Shangri-La. She finally managed to tear her gaze away and looked up to the man beside her, who stood tall and proud. 'It's…spectacular. I had no idea.'

He looked down to the ground and gestured for her to look too. She saw a clump of the most beautiful flowers she'd ever seen. They were vibrant pink with four large pointy-tipped petals.

Nadim said, 'That's the desert rose—native to here. The land blooms with them for months after the rains, and then they fade away just before the rains come again next summer.' He looked at her then. 'This is one of the best vantage points to see Merkazad.'

Overcome with some nameless emotion, Iseult looked at the view again and said huskily, 'Thank you for showing me this.'

She'd always thought of herself as a home bird, but she had to admit that she hadn't felt homesick here at all. It was as if her heart had skipped a beat and gone on at a different rhythm, and she knew how easy it would be to be seduced by this land.

She felt a light yet burning touch on her bare elbow. She looked up to see Nadim's dark eyes staring down into hers, and in that moment everyone and all the vehicles around them disappeared. She knew it wasn't just the land she was in danger of being seduced by; it was this man. And she was quite sure he wasn't *trying* to seduce her!

'Come—you will travel the rest of the journey with me.'

And with just the slightest inclination of his head the man who had been sharing the back seat of his chauffeur-driven Jeep got out and took Iseult's place where she had been. She was guided into the back of Nadim's Jeep. She doubted very much that even if she had protested she would have been listened to.

She sat tensely in the plush confines of Nadim's Jeep, with his big body far too close for comfort, and blurted out, 'Why are you bringing me with you?'

He turned his head to look at her, and the breath shrivelled up in her throat. In his turban and traditional robes he looked so...exotic and otherworldly.

He quirked a small mocking smile. 'I'm bringing you along because I value your opinion, of course.'

Iseult all but snorted inelegantly, and partly to escape his dark penetrating gaze said, 'I doubt that. You probably just don't trust that I can be left to my own devices for a weekend.'

'You're right about that.'

Iseult turned to look at him again, full of chagrin and fire, but before she could speak he was saying, '*But* I also do happen to wonder what you'll make of the horses we'll see here. Most are not worth bothering about, but sometimes there are some fine pure-blood Arabians.'

Slightly mollified, but still feeling very confused and out of her comfort zone, Iseult nevertheless felt a spark of interest pique her. She asked him about the Arabian horses, and before she knew it she had twisted fully in the seat to face him. They were talking so intensely that she didn't even notice when they'd come to a halt.

The driver opened Iseult's door, and she got out to see the most magical sight laid out before her. They were high in the mountains in an ancient-looking village—a cluster of buildings nestled around them. They all seemed to be made out of hard-packed red clay. Men, women and children had come to a standstill to see the Sheikh—*their* Sheikh—arrive.

One of the men, with a white skullcap on his head, darted forward to greet Nadim, who had come around to Iseult's side of the Jeep. Nadim gestured autocratically for Iseult to follow him, and with the bodyguards crowding around her and Nadim she had no choice.

With wide eyes she took in the scene: tall palm trees swayed in the light breeze, and beyond the village she could see that there was a flat lush greenness all around them, surrounded by craggy mountains. In the distance she could see a large

area which had huge crowds milling around and
tents erected.

Iseult caught up with Nadim. 'What is this
place? Where are we?'

He cast her a quick glance. 'This is al Sahar,
the tribal home of my ancestors. These are my
people...literally. The al Saqrs are descended
from the Bedouin warrior people who roamed this
land for hundreds of years. It's a mountain oasis,
fed from the springs that are abundant after the
monsoons.'

Iseult could see that they were approaching some
lavish-looking tents, and saw too that Lina was
entering a small tent with Iseult's things. Nadim
stopped and Iseult nearly ran into his back. She
stepped back hurriedly, her face flushing.

He gestured to the small tent Lina had just disappeared into. 'That is your lodgings. I have business
to discuss with village leaders and Bedouin visitors. Someone will bring you to the horse enclosure where the sales and races are going on. I'll
meet you there later.'

And with that, and a flick of his robes, he was
gone, taking his whole retinue with him, leaving
Iseult standing there stupidly.

Lina popped her head out of the heavily draped
velvet curtains. 'Miss Iseult...'

Iseult went in, and her eyes had to adjust to the
dim light after the bright sunlight. And then her

eyes widened. She'd walked into a scene straight out of *One Thousand and One Nights*. Richly embroidered carpets littered the floor in a haphazard clash of luxurious colour, and dominating the small space was a bed which seemed to be made entirely out of sumptuous velvet and silk cushions. Beautifully intricate chairs and a table were in another corner, and Lina was showing her where a softly draped curtain hid a changing and washing area.

Once again she felt like asking if they were in the right place, but Lina was already busy unpacking Iseult's things. Iseult couldn't have felt more out of place in her dusty jeans, T-shirt and scuffed riding boots.

Lina hurried to the opening of the tent and said to Iseult, 'Jamal is here now. He will take you to the horses…'

Almost glad to get away from the slightly oppressive feeling of being hemmed in by such opulence, Iseult hurried out to where a shy young man waited. He led her towards where the crowds were milling. She could see that it was mainly men, and they turned to look at her curiously as she came through. Many more tents had been erected nearby, although none as lavish as hers and what she assumed to be Nadim's. In clusters around the tents she saw women, busy preparing food and washing.

There were many enclosures. Some with horses, some with camels. In the distance she could see that a camel race was taking place. Jamal, her guide, seemed to be happy for her to wander around, so she did so for a couple of hours. Interspersed with the horses and camels were some women selling colourful pottery and jewellery. Iseult smiled apologetically, because she had no money, and vowed to come back and buy some things later or the following day.

Moving away, she came to a few enclosures that held just one or two horses with serious-looking men discussing them. She could see instantly that these were a superior breed to the other horses and her heart quickened. All the modern thoroughbred horses around the world were supposedly descended from three Arabian stallions, and looking at these particular horses now Iseult could see why.

There was one in particular which caught her eye, on its own. She could sense that it was a little wild. She'd seen some of the men trot horses bareback around the enclosures, so Iseult didn't think much before she was about to climb over the fence and have a closer look at this stallion.

Just as she was about to lift her leg over she felt herself being pulled back. Knowing it couldn't be the shy Jamal, and knowing full well who it was just by the way his touch seemed to sear right through her, she swung back down to see Nadim glaring down at her.

'What do you think you're doing?'

Iseult squared up to him. 'I was just going to take a closer look at a horse—that's why you brought me here, isn't it?'

He seemed to look at her for a long time, and then a muscle twitched in his jaw. 'He's not saddled.'

'I was riding horses bareback before I learnt how to ride in a saddle.'

Another long moment passed, and then he said, 'Very well. But you don't go in there without a hat.'

Iseult all but rolled her eyes. None of the men trying out the other horses was wearing a hat. But remembering his wife's accident kept her quiet and suddenly subdued. In an instant Jamal returned and handed Iseult a hard hat. She slapped it on her head and tied it securely, and gave Nadim a look that had his eyes flashing dangerously.

Iseult took a box over to where the horse stood and, using it to gain height, vaulted easily onto its back. He was skittish, but soon calmed down, and she could feel the sleek power of his muscles move beneath her as she made him go into a light trot.

Nadim watched Iseult ride the stallion, and was aware of every other man watching her too. A hush had fallen over the crowd. He'd never seen someone ride a horse with such ease and effortless grace. Her long hair trailed down her back from under the hat like a living flame of colour. And the line of her back was as straight as a dancer's. Her whole carriage was that of a regal queen, and he was reminded of that first moment he'd seen her on Devil's Kiss in Ireland. One hand rested nonchalantly on her thigh, the other on the horses's reins.

She was his. The assertion ran through him, stunning him with its force. He could see that she was about to come to a halt, and had a moment of premonition before he realised that a horse race was about to start in the distance. Suddenly the loud crack of a starter pistol rent the air.

All Iseult knew was that she was about to dismount when a huge burst of sound made the horse rear into the air. With nothing but flimsy reins to hold onto she was thrown off like a rag doll. Landing on her back, she felt the wind knocked out of her, and she struggled to regain breath. Just in that instant a huge dark shape appeared, and she felt the hat being gently pulled off her head. Then hands were everywhere—probing her head, neck, shoulders and ribs with an expert touch.

She wanted to smack the hands away, but she was too weak and they were too insistent. Finally she managed to take in a big sucking breath of air. She struggled to sit up, but big hands kept her down. Suddenly the aches and pains she could feel starting to register were nothing compared to the fact that Nadim loomed above her, with his hands all over her.

Finally she managed to knock away his hands, protesting breathlessly, 'I'm fine. I've been thrown a million times before.'

Nadim was livid. Iseult could see that. 'Yes, but not on ground like this. It could break your back.'

She struggled to sit up, and Nadim helped her. Iseult looked into his grim face. His hands were still on her arms. Guilt flooded her. 'I'm sorry,' she said immediately, thinking of his wife.

Her expressive face must have given her away, because Nadim said grimly, 'This is completely different.'

Remorse flooded Iseult as she tried to stand awkwardly. Of course it was. Even if he hadn't loved his wife, he must have had great affection for her. Not to mention his unborn child. And she... she was nothing to this man but an irritation he couldn't seem to help himself from kissing when the mood took him.

This view was compounded when he lifted Iseult up into his arms before she knew what was happening, and strode out of the enclosure saying caustically, 'I swear your middle name is trouble.'

Ridiculously, tears threatened, and Iseult had

to blink rapidly to ease the burn. Her throat was clogged. She couldn't even protest and ask to be put down, and it felt all too devastating to be held like this against Nadim's broad and hard chest as he cut a swathe through the gawping crowd. The material of his *thobe* was silk and felt ridiculously flimsy. The heat from his body was making her skin tingle all over.

He brought her to his Jeep, which was nearby, and placed her in the back. Closing her door, he went around and got in the other side. Iseult tried to say something, and hated the way her voice sounded so thready. 'You don't have to do this. I can walk back. It's not far from here.'

She even put her hand on the handle of the door, and Nadim barked out, '*Woman*, will you just stay put!' He put an arm across her belly, stopping her from getting out, and Iseult could feel emotion welling again.

She was barely breathing, begging silently for Nadim to take his arm away as the Jeep started to move. Clenching her jaw to keep the emotion down, she resolutely looked out of the window to avoid more censure.

She heard a deep sigh and his arm was gone— but only for a hand to come to her chin and turn her face to his. Iseult heard him mutter something that sounded guttural and foreign. To her utter horror and chagrin, tears flooded her eyes. Nadim cursed again and took out a handkerchief, handing it to Iseult.

She took it warily and blew her nose.

'I'm sorry, I didn't mean to make you cry…are you hurt?'

Iseult shook her head and blinked back the tears, swallowing. 'No…just a bit bruised, I think. On my back.'

'Show me…' His voice was more gentle than she'd ever heard it, nearly undoing her again.

Iseult didn't know what was happening until Nadim had nudged her forward on the seat so that he could pull up her T-shirt to look. 'What are you doing?' she demanded. But he paid no heed, and his muttered words told her that she must have a few glorious bruises already blooming. Her bottom felt as if it had taken most of the impact, but the thought of him looking down there made her go hot all over.

Nadim set her back, and to her surprise he couldn't meet her eyes. He said stiffly, 'I should never have brought you here or let you get on that horse. I thought he looked too skittish.'

'I'm fine—honestly. I bruise easily, so it probably looks worse than it is. It's nothing a hot bath won't cure. And you wouldn't have known how skittish he was unless someone had got on his back.'

Nadim cast her a grim look. 'Yes, but it didn't

have to be you. That's what those boys are there for. They're hardy and well able to handle horses like that.'

Iseult bit her tongue, knowing Nadim wouldn't welcome a heated defence right now. The Jeep came to a stop and Iseult could see Lina hovering anxiously. Had word reached her already? She opened the Jeep door and winced when she felt her back protest. Nadim was there, and she saw his face darken ominously. He rapped out instructions to Lina and helped Iseult from the Jeep.

When she was out, he said, 'Lina will take care of you and see to those bruises. You should rest this evening.'

And then he was handing her to Lina and stepping away abruptly. Iseult felt bereft, and wanted to protest that she'd be fine, not wanting to miss out on anything. There was an air of suppressed excitement around the camp as a group of black-clad giggling women went past, but she knew better now than to push Nadim, so just said meekly, 'All right.'

Lina wouldn't leave even when Iseult protested that she'd be fine. She drew her a bath, and when Iseult sank her aching body into it, it was like slipping into warm silk. Lina had added all sorts of oils, and even rose blossoms floated on the fragrant water. With her hair piled high onto her head she sank back, and had to admit that she'd never experienced something so decadently sensual.

Suddenly at the thought of that word *sensual* she felt ridiculous, and sat up as if to get out. Immediately a stern-eyed Lina was there. 'You stay in the bath, Miss Iseult. You need to let the healing oils work.'

Iseult sank back down hurriedly—as much because she'd never been naked before someone else as anything else. 'Okay,' she said sheepishly, but then added, 'But only if you stop calling me Miss Iseult…it's Iseult.'

Iseult could see from Lina's dark eyes that she was smiling, and wondered what she looked like. 'Okay, Miss Iseult.'

She left her alone again, and when Iseult was starting to feel like a prune, she reappeared, holding a large towel. Iseult got out and Lina wrapped her in the towel. After she'd dried herself Lina appeared again with a pot of ointment, and smoothed the cream into her tender back and buttocks. Then she draped a robe of some sort over a nearby chair and bade Iseult goodnight.

Iseult dropped the towel and drew on the robe. It was made of brushed silk, and felt far too delicate for someone like her. An edging of gold thread went around its whole perimeter. There was a long golden ribbon-like tie which ran just under her breasts, and she looked up from tying it to see herself reflected in a mirror in the washing area.

She was caught unawares, and stood transfixed by the unfamiliar person reflected back at her. In the mirror was a woman with a long graceful neck, highlighted by the hair piled high on her head. Her eyes were huge, her mouth full and pink. She looked pale, her skin almost luminous in the low lights. She looked very nearly...*beautiful*.

With a shaking hand Iseult reached up and undid her hair, so that it fell down her back and over her shoulders. With one hand on the tie under her breasts, and the other falling limply to her side, she couldn't stop looking. She'd been transformed into someone else. *The person she felt stirring within her when Nadim kissed her.*

The material fell in a diaphanous swirl of cream and gold to her feet, skimming over curves she'd never thought she had, making them look fuller, more alluring. The generous shape of her breasts she'd always fought to hide was accentuated by the deep V and empire line of the robe, with her cleavage a shadowy line between them.

She looked...she looked like— She heard a sound then, and the breath left her throat. Her skin tingled and the hairs stood up on the back of her neck. Hoping against hope it was just Lina, but knowing exactly who it was, she turned to see that Nadim had come to the entrance of the tent.

He was dressed in dark gold robes now, and Iseult could see that the sun was setting outside, just beyond his turbaned head and broad shoulders. Every cell in her body reacted violently at seeing him there, and she was caught in such a vulnerable moment she could only look at him helplessly.

Nadim fought to remember why he'd come to Iseult's tent; perhaps it had been some bid to assure himself that he *could* resist her, and that he should keep trying to resist her—because she was an employee, and because he knew that beneath that spiky exterior she was vulnerable and had shouldered a heavy burden for a long time. She wasn't worldly, like the mistresses he was careful to take now—women who knew the score. No emotional involvement. He could end up hurting Iseult, just as he'd hurt his own wife…

Despite all those very good reasons he fought to try and say something, anything coherent, and not just stand there like a teenager transfixed by the first naked woman he'd ever seen.

And she wasn't even naked! But the delicate robe might as well have been see-through. The line of her cleavage still looked damp, the skin pale and silky-looking next to the material. And through the fall of the robe he could see those long long legs, and in between them the shadowy promise of a carnal satisfaction he'd never craved this badly before… It made his blood thrum and his body harden in rampant response.

'How is your back?' It was a miracle he'd found his voice. Nadim didn't dare even move one inch towards Iseult, knowing that if he did he wouldn't re-emerge from that tent until he'd had her. And the gut-clenching panic he'd felt when he'd seen that horse throw her like a rag-doll still made him feel very vulnerable. Too vulnerable.

Iseult blinked and suddenly felt cold. For a moment there— She mentally shook her head and was instantly self-conscious. She was practically naked! She crossed her arms to cover her breasts, unaware of how it pushed them forward, or of how the robe gaped slightly, showing a long length of leg. She was also unaware of how Nadim tensed, because he was cast in shadow.

'Fine… Lina gave me some ointment…'

Nadim just inclined his head. 'Good. Lina comes from a family of healers, so you're in good hands. But you'll probably be sore tomorrow.'

Iseult shook her head. 'Really. I'm fine. I'm sure you have to be somewhere…?'

He nodded once abruptly. 'Goodnight, then, Iseult.'

'Goodnight.'

Of course he had somewhere else to be, a voice mocked her. He left, and seemed to suck the energy of the space out with him. Iseult sagged, literally, against the chair, and a wave of humiliation washed through her to think of how she'd been mooning at herself in the mirror, believing that she was looking at someone different. Believing she might be beautiful. *Feminine.* Believing that perhaps he'd brought her here because of something elemental that had passed between them that morning on the terrace.

She was no different from the girl who had never been feminine—the girl her classmates had found it so easy to send up. And she would never be anything else. She would never be the kind of woman to have a man like Nadim. They were worlds and leagues apart, and clearly he just felt some misguided sense of responsibility towards her.

With an inarticulate sound of rage at herself, she tore off the robe, hearing it tear.

Tears pricked her eyes as she found and pulled on the pants and T-shirt she normally slept in. Castigating herself bitterly for her weakness, she crawled into the sumptuous bed, suddenly wishing she were back at home in Kildare and sliding between plain flannel sheets—not these silky decadent sheets that made her think of Nadim and want hot, forbidden things.

CHAPTER EIGHT

THE following day Iseult was up and dressed in her usual uniform of jeans and a shirt and riding boots. Ready and waiting to take on the day and ignore her disturbing growing feelings for Nadim. Without waiting for instruction she went back to the horse enclosure, to the same horse that had thrown her off the day before.

Determined to prove something to herself as much as anyone else, she put on a hat and got onto his back to conquer the fleeting fear that such a fall always engendered.

Nadim watched Iseult from a distance and shook his head ruefully. He knew she hadn't seen him yet as that telltale tension in her body whenever he came near hadn't come into her. At that moment he knew that any hope of control over this attraction was futile. He'd thought somewhat misguidedly that he might be able to wait until the Sultan of Al-Omar's birthday party next week, but even the prospect of looking at another woman was anathema to him now.

He grimaced at the thought of a day of meetings ahead, and celebrations in his honour tonight, but even with aides clamouring for his attention Nadim didn't move away until he saw that Iseult was safely off the horse.

That evening Iseult could feel the aches and pains from her fall the day before making themselves known again. She'd been aware of Nadim at a distance all day, but he'd made no attempt to come and talk to her, staying deep in discussion with the group of men who followed him around. She felt a little bereft to think that he undoubtedly regretted bringing her and had no further use for her.

Lina had served Iseult dinner in the tent, and had told her that she and some of the other women were due to perform a traditional Bedouin dance for Sheikh Nadim and his guests that night so she had to get ready. She was leaving now, and a sudden fear gripped Iseult that Nadim would materialise again and send her flimsy control to pieces. On an impulse she asked Lina if she could come and watch her get ready.

Lina hesitated for a moment, and then with sparkling eyes nodded, taking Iseult by the hand and leading her out to another small tent nearby. Once inside, Iseult could see about a dozen women. She smiled shyly at them and watched as Lina took off her *burka*, revealing a luxurious fall of black hair to her waist and an extraordinarily pretty face.

Lina giggled at Iseult's reaction and got ready, revealing that under her long *abeyya* she had been wearing jeans and a T-shirt. Fascinated, Iseult sat down cross-legged in a corner and watched as the girls and women took turns to get each other ready. Lina had disappeared behind a screen, and when she emerged again Iseult was shocked after having seen so little flesh bared up till now. She was dressed in silk and chiffon harem pants with ornate ankle bracelets, and her hair was plaited in a shining rope of black against her back.

A short-sleeved top exposed her belly and hips, and she had gold rings up her arms and a gold chain around her curvaceous waist. A veil was secured at the back of her head, which she pulled across her face above her nose, obscuring her features again.

One of the other girls giggled and said something to Lina, who looked at Iseult with a mischievous expression. Iseult saw her advance and knew that look. She started to protest even as Lina reached down and pulled her up with both hands. Before Iseult knew what was happening she was being administered to by a dozen women, all intent on getting her dressed exactly as they were.

Iseult protested again, but to no avail; they were

determined, and as she had no idea what to expect she gave herself up to the experience, telling herself they were just having fun. Soon she was dressed exactly like the others, and Lina was fastening a gold chain around her waist. She felt all at once naked and exhilarated.

Lina stood back and clapped her hands. 'Miss Iseult, now you're one of us!'

Iseult smiled weakly, and mentally compared her own milk-bottle-white skin to the glorious olive of the girls around her. She felt completely exposed in the brief silk top. Her breasts were bigger than the other girls', and she was all but spilling from the low neckline. But there was something decadently sensual about the trousers sitting on her hips and the gold chain around her waist. A long veil was attached to her own hair, which Lina had coiled down her back, and she showed her how to cover her face from view.

For a brief moment she was transported back to the previous evening, when she'd caught sight of her reflection in the mirror. But there was no mirror or Nadim here to break the spell being woven around her as one of the other girls knelt at her feet and fastened ankle bracelets. She'd never experienced this girly camaraderie of dressing up and it was heady.

Thinking that they were just having fun before they went to perform, she was completely unprepared when Lina took her hand again. Suddenly they were all on the move.

'Wait, where are we going?' she asked.

Lina looked back. 'We're one dancer short… Just stay behind me and copy what I do—you'll be fine!'

Her cry of, *'But I've never danced in my life!'* got lost as the girls flitted like exotically beautiful ghosts through the inky twilight between the tents. Iseult desperately covered her face with the veil, and sent up a silent prayer that Nadim wouldn't recognise her. If he did…she shivered inwardly… he'd kill her for sure.

They stood at the back of a huge tent, where lots of men sat on cushions in groups around low tables piled high with food and drinks. Iseult's heart was thumping when she saw a long line of men at the top, with Nadim right in the centre, looking stern and austere in black robes. They made him look even more dark and gorgeous. *And dangerous.*

The beat of a drum started nearby—a seductive beat of another world. Iseult watched as the other girls started to move out amongst the tables, lifting their arms high and moving their veils back and forth, alternately revealing and hiding themselves, hips moving in a primal rhythm to the drums.

They went out two by two, and then Lina was moving and taking Iseult with her. Iseult had no choice but to follow, and concentrated desperately on copying Lina's movements—the small steps she took, the way her hips swayed with such effortless sensuality. She knew she was nowhere near emulating her.

They were dangerously close to the top of the room now, just feet away from Nadim, and Iseult had the veil clutched tight across her face above her nose. She could feel the warm evening air skate over her bared midriff, and knew it would take a miracle for him not to notice her pale skin.

Even so, despite her fear of being caught, Iseult couldn't help the way the beat of the drums seemed to ignite a fire in her blood, and following Lina was very mesmeric. As if determined to thwart her best efforts, though, she found herself darting a quick glance to the big dark presence just a few feet away.

Nadim sat with one leg propped up and an arm resting on his knee. And he was looking right at her with a dark, blistering gaze that tore strips off her skin. Iseult nearly stumbled, but somehow managed to keep going, ripping her eyes away from Nadim.

To her intense relief Lina was moving towards the back of the room, where the other girls were in a huddle, giggling. Iseult tried to reassure herself that Nadim hadn't known it was her; he couldn't really have noticed in the dimly lit tent. The drums were still beating, and with shock at what she'd just done setting in Iseult took a step outside to gulp in big breaths of air. She was shaking all over.

Just then, out of nowhere, came a movement so quick and overpowering it took her completely by surprise. She was being lifted off her feet against a wall of steel, with one arm just below her breasts and a big hand over her mouth. As if she weighed no more than a bag of sugar her captor strode away with her into the shadows.

CHAPTER NINE

ISEULT kicked her legs uselessly into thin air and tried to scream—but of course she couldn't get a sound out. The most terrifying thing was that she knew exactly who it was, because the wall of steel against her back felt incredibly familiar. She'd felt it that day in the dining room at home in Ireland. And suddenly it wasn't terror she was feeling but a wild excitement.

Iseult put her hands up to try and claw his hand down from her mouth but he was immovable. She saw that they were approaching a big tent, set apart from the others, with two tall lamps holding burning flames at its entrance. In scant seconds they were through the heavy drapes at the entrance and Iseult was summarily dropped to her feet.

She whirled around to face her captor, breathing harshly. Her heart thumped violently to see Nadim so tall and dark and intimidating. Any angry words she'd articulated in her head disappeared as she realised that she was half naked. Her body felt as if it was on fire under Nadim's still blistering gaze.

He bit out caustically, 'Were you born into this world with a mission in life to drive me completely insane?'

Iseult was coping with too many things at once— not least of which was the fact that her heaving breasts felt as if they were about to pop out of her top—so she just said shakily, 'You took me out of my world and into yours, so if I'm driving you mad you only have yourself to blame.'

He almost flinched, as if she'd hit a nerve. 'I knew it was a mistake to bring you here.'

Hurt and anger lanced Iseult at hearing his bitter words, seeing his undeniable reaction of regret. 'Well, then, why don't you just send me home and out of your hair once and for all?'

Iseult made as if to move around him to leave, but Nadim caught her by her bare upper arm. She stopped, still breathing raggedly. She wouldn't look up into that harsh, beautiful face.

His voice sounded guttural, hoarse. 'I can't let you go because to send you away would drive my insanity to another level entirely. You're in my blood now, Iseult.'

Slowly her head lifted, and she looked up at Nadim and stopped breathing when she saw the heated intensity in his eyes. 'Wh-what are you talking about?'

He brought her round so she stood in front of him again, and with his free hand tore the turban off his head and threw it into a corner. He suddenly looked much younger, and unbearably rakish. 'I want you. I've wanted you since the moment I saw you.'

Iseult's legs turned to jelly. She fought not to let herself be swept away by a rising tide of desire. 'I won't let you kiss me again just because you feel like it, only to cast me aside as if *I've* done something wrong.'

Nadim moved closer, both hands on her arms now. Iseult was finding it hard to breathe or stay clear-headed. He shook his head, eyes burning down into hers. 'I've tried staying away from you but I can't any more. It's making me crazy. I'm not even going to ask how you ended up dancing with Lina. Every time I turn around you're doing the unexpected... When I saw you appear before me in that excuse of an outfit any control I may have had disappeared... I need to know now—do you want this too?'

Iseult looked up at Nadim. Just inches separated them from bodily contact. Their breaths were already mingling. Her breasts felt full and aching against the tight top, and she had the curious sensation of the real world slipping away. Here in this dim light, in the ornate and luxurious surroundings of Nadim's tent, they could have been transported back one hundred years in time to another world.

Nadim looked like a warrior king, his jaw tight, the planes of his face austerely gorgeous as he waited to hear her answer. Everything that had happened between them was crytallised in this moment. And Iseult knew what she was going to say with a bone-deep feeling of rightness.

Yes.

It rose from deep within her, with an inexorable flooding of heat into her body. She was no more capable of denying she wanted him, than she was of surviving another second without breathing.

'Yes...' she said faintly, huskily. 'I want this too...'

With a perceptible tremor in his hands that surprised Iseult, and comforted her on some very vulnerable level, Nadim pulled her closer until their bodies were touching. Suddenly Jamilah's warning words came back to her: *The al Saqr men can be ruthless in their pursuit, and equally ruthless when they're finished with you.*

But in that moment Nadim's head was lowering, that unbearably sensuous mouth was coming closer and closer, and it was very easy for Iseult to block the words out.

When Nadim's mouth settled over hers it felt as though time had slowed down to a drip-drip of sensual delight. He kissed her with such languorous intent, exploring softly, teasing, tasting, biting down gently on her full lower lip, before coming back to settle over her mouth again with a hint of barely leashed passion.

That tipped Iseult over the precarious edge she'd been clinging onto even unbeknown to herself, and with a faint moan she leant closer into him, her arms climbing up to twine around his neck.

And as if Nadim hadn't entirely trusted her words, but had been waiting for a tacit signal, he drew her even closer, so that the space now between their beating hearts was non-existent. His tongue made a bold foray into Iseult's mouth and she welcomed it, welcomed him, her tongue shyly touching and tasting.

Passion quickly blazed up around them. Iseult was barely aware of Nadim flicking away the veil from the back of her head. His hands were on her bare hips, pulling her in even closer, where she was dimly aware of something hard digging into her belly. Belated realisation of what it must be had her pulling back for a moment to look down. Nadim followed her gaze to where his ornate dagger was still tucked into his rope belt.

He quirked a sexy smile. 'I don't think we'll need that.'

Mouth dry, Iseult watched as he pulled it out. About to throw it aside, he seemed to reconsider. He pulled it from its scabard and with one hand turned Iseult so that her back faced him. She shivered slightly, but with anticipation, not fear. She felt him pull her hair aside, so that it hung over one shoulder, and then he pulled the back of her top taut. The cold edge of the blade touched against her skin for the tiniest moment, and then suddenly the tightness of her top was released and air whistled over her naked back.

With a sucked-in breath of shock and excitement Iseult brought her hands to her breasts, holding the top in place. She heard the dull thud of the knife falling somewhere, and then Nadim's big hands were smoothing the rent sides of the short top apart, and she felt his breath feathering before he started to press kisses from her neck down her spine.

Iseult's head fell forward, her heart thumping wildly as she felt Nadim's hands settle on her hips, fingers curving around to her soft belly as his mouth travelled back up to her neck and shoulder, nudging the ripped side of her top down over one shoulder.

She had no experience, but Iseult felt some deeply innate feminine instinct kick in at that moment. So when Nadim turned her around gently to face him again she looked up, straight into his eyes, and fell into two pools of dark sensual promise. Any hint of remaining doubt fled.

Staring deep into her eyes, mesmerising her, he

let his hands come to the shoulders of her top and tug softly. Iseult's hands impeded the process, still welded as they were across her breasts.

'Trust me...' Nadim said, and with a slightly choked breath Iseult let her hands drop. The top gaped, and Nadim's eyes left hers to look down as the stiff silk material was finally pulled away and down her arms, baring her to his hot gaze.

Iseult trembled. Her breasts felt heavy and aching, her nipples tight and hard, prickling with sensation. The ruined top fell to the floor. Iseult saw Nadim's face flush, his jaw tighten. He reached out a dark hand and cupped the heavy weight of her breast. She had to bite back a moan and couldn't look down, knowing that she might collapse altogether if she saw the darkness of his skin against the paleness of hers.

'You're so beautiful...' he breathed, and before Iseult's inner demons had time to rise his thumb had found her nipple and brushed back and forth, teasing it to even further tingling tightness. This time she nearly did fall, and on a reflex put out her hands to his arms in an effort to stay standing.

The movement caused her breast to press into his hand fully, and even holding onto him couldn't keep Iseult upright any more. In an instant Nadim had bent and lifted her into his arms, and carried her over to a sumptuously clothed bed.

He laid her down as reverentially as if she were

made of china and then stood back. All Iseult could do was look up, dry-mouthed, as Nadim started to disrobe. The heavy outer robe fell to the ground, the rope belt came off, and in a split second the dark *thobe* had disappeared.

Iseult's gaze fell to take in the magnificence of his broad chest, leanly muscled and olive skinned, two blunt dark nipples standing amongst a fine sprinkling of dark hair.

Her eyes dropped to the low slung waist of his under-trousers, loose, but not loose enough to disguise the prominent bulge. Cheeks flaming, Iseult lifted her eyes again and saw Nadim's riveted on her. Feeling self-conscious, she brought up an arm over her breasts.

And then he was there, beside her, one hand removing her arm from her breasts, brushing against a sensitive nipple. He stretched her arm up, over her head, where his fingers interlaced with hers, holding her captive.

He bent his head and feathered a kiss to her mouth. 'Don't hide yourself from me...'

A heated languor melted through Iseult's veins, and yet at the same time she felt more energised than she'd ever felt, with a dull, throbbing ache setting up in her lower belly and between her legs.

With a slowness she was sure was meant to drive her insane, Nadim traced his other hand and fingers around her breast, moulding the fleshy contour before cupping it and squeezing gently, so that the hard tip stood out like an enticement.

With a wicked gleam in his eyes, still holding one hand captive, he bent again and pressed hot open-mouthed kisses all down her chest, between the valley of her breasts, and then after a screaming second of torture he licked around the aureole and dragged that hot, tingling tip into his mouth.

Iseult's back arched as if she'd been electrocuted. She'd never felt anything like it in her life, and she squeezed her legs together reflexively to stem the tide of liquid heat. Her fingers clasped Nadim's in a death grip, and her other hand funnelled through his silky hair, keeping his head and that wicked mouth in place.

He moved to the other breast, administering the same torture, making Iseult gasp out loud and suck in short breaths. He finally released her other hand and drew back slightly, but only to look his fill. Iseult felt wanton and uncontrollable. Her nipples were wet from his mouth and tongue, his cheeks flushed, eyes glittering.

'Nadim…' she husked, not even knowing what she was asking for.

Nadim had to pause for a moment. For the first time in his life he felt out of control with a woman. Heat and lust had morphed together, clouding his brain in a searing heat haze, and all he wanted to do was bury himself so far and deep into Iseult's slick body that he knew if he didn't impose some control he'd hurt her.

But it was near impossible to regain that control. Her breasts were like two succulent fruits, her back still slightly arched. When he'd felt that spasmodic response as he'd closed his mouth around one hard, tight nipple and sucked it deep, he'd damn near exploded. She was biting her lip now, her eyes glazed, dark golden pools of desire…her hair was spread out around her in glorious disarray.

Smoothing his hands down the sides of her body, out over the gentle swell of her hips, he snagged on the ties of her skimpy harem pants. With little more than a tug they were gone, falling away in a diaphanous cloud by the bed, taking her panties with them.

Now she lay there with nothing except the gold chain around her waist and the gold ankle bracelets, and Nadim did not have the spatial ability to even attempt removing those. Feeling suddenly constricted, he stood and dispensed with his own trousers. He saw Iseult's gaze drop and her cheeks pale slightly when she saw the sheer evidence of his arousal…

Iseult knew all about sex, even if she'd never had it. She'd watched stallions mount mares all her life, so she knew all about the earthy reality. But to see Nadim fully naked and fully aroused intimidated her more than she cared to admit. Any thought of telling him she was a virgin fled her mind. They'd gone too far now, and even as she balked at his physicality she knew she didn't want to turn back. If he knew she was a virgin...

Nadim came down on the bed alongside Iseult, scattering her thoughts. He lay on his side and with a possessive arm pulled her into him. She breathed in the musky scent of their arousal. She could feel his erection pressing against her and it made her want to move her hips. Any trepidation fled.

Tentatively she trailed a shy hand up over his lean waist and torso, watching how his belly was sucked in on a short breath. Her fingers found a hard blunt nipple, and acting on pure instinct she bent down and found it with her mouth, kissing it before biting and nipping gently, savouring the salty taste of his skin, running a hand down his back to the indent just above his firm buttocks.

Nadim fisted a hand in her hair and pulled her head back up. Pressed torso to torso, length to length, they touched everywhere. With an enigmatic look that Iseult couldn't decipher Nadim covered her mouth with his in a searing kiss and pulled her even closer, his arms wrapped around her so tight that her breasts were flattened against his chest. She didn't even know where he ended and she began.

An urgency was building between her legs and in her belly, a tightening coil of tension, and Iseult moved restlessly, unwittingly causing stars and spots to explode behind Nadim's eyes as he fought to retain control.

Nadim's hands smoothed down her back, down to her bottom, pulling her into him even more. Instinctively Iseult opened her legs, feeling Nadim's heated erection sliding between them. Hearts were thumping out of control, and Iseult felt a light sweat break out all over her skin. She'd never been so intent on one thing: reaching an elusive peak with this man.

In an effortless move Nadim shifted them so that Iseult was flat on her back and he lay between her legs. She could feel the potent strength of him between her thighs, but still he didn't move. He just bent his head and found her mouth again, drugging her with his kisses.

She heard the faint sound of foil ripping, and there was a moment when Nadim pulled back. She opened her eyes with a faint mewl of despair. She needed something right now that only he could give her. She wrapped her hands around his biceps, feeling them bunch and move under silky-smooth skin.

Her legs moved further apart even as her thighs gripped his lean waist, and she felt him move down slightly. He touched her intimately with one finger, drawing it slowly up the desire-drenched folds of her sex, finding where the evidence of her arousal

was a hard swell of nerve-endings and rubbing her
there.

Iseult's back arched again. Pressing herself
into his hand, she couldn't breathe, couldn't think
straight. Her hands gripped his arms so tight
that she thought she'd leave him with permanent
marks.

'Nadim…' she said hoarsely, desperately. *'Please…'*

'What?' he asked, all innocence wrapped up in
the devil, and he continued to tease her with his
finger, which was moving inside her now, where
she felt slick and hot.

'I could tease you and watch you all night, but
not any more… I can't wait…'

Before Iseult knew what was happening, or had
sucked in a breath, Nadim was pushing himself
into her. Filling her, stretching her…impossibly.
She gasped for a moment, and jerked her hips as
if to move away from his penetration, but even as
she did she could feel a glorious friction.

Nadim frowned down at her. 'Iseult…are you…?'

Iseult somehow knew the discomfort would be
fleeting. She reached up and pulled his head down,
pulling him closer, and wrapped her legs around
his waist.

'Don't stop. Please don't stop, Nadim…' She saw
him wage what looked to be an intense inner battle,
before he made an inarticulate sound and said gut-
turally, 'Relax…this might hurt for a moment…'

Iseult looked up into his eyes, telling him silently that she trusted him implicitly, and in that moment she did. She could feel him flex his bottom, and then he thrust in, making her breath catch at the searing, burning pain.

Immediately his mouth was on hers, kissing her, drugging her as she felt him go deeper. And the pain was fading magically, and as he started to pull out again she felt that delicious friction. Loath to let him go, she moved her hips with him, but then he came back, thrusting in again, even deeper this time.

Iseult's legs were locked around his waist, her chest arched up to his and her head falling back as she struggled to comprehend all the sensations running through her body and head.

Nadim brought a hand around her back, arching her up even more, and thrust again, deeper, a little harder. Iseult moaned. She felt his breath feather over her hot skin and gasped out loud when he took a nipple deep into his mouth, swirling his tongue around it, biting gently as he took up a remorseless rhythm, driving in and out of her body.

The intensity of sensation was overwhelming. Iseult could only cling onto Nadim. He was her anchor, the centre of her universe, and he was threatening to topple her over an edge she'd never known before. But with him looking down into her eyes she was fearless.

His strokes got longer, deeper and faster, and Iseult felt her muscles clenching. She was rushing headlong into something she could only guess at, and in that moment everything exploded around her, and a carnal pleasure she'd never even imagined existed pulsed through her even as Nadim still moved in and out.

Iseult could feel her muscles spasm along his hard length, but she couldn't articulate anything, knowing that she must look shocked. She felt shocked. What she'd just experienced had reformed all her cells into a new configuration, and this man's stamp was all over them.

As she watched Nadim's eyes closed tight, his head was flung back, the veins of his neck stood out. And with one final powerful thrust he stilled, and the only sound that could be heard was their laboured breathing.

Iseult was still floating in a limbo land of half-consciousness when she felt herself being lifted out of the bed by strong arms. She murmured something and felt Nadim's breath close to her ear. His deep husky voice sent a frisson of remembered ecstasy through her. 'Shh, I've run you a bath… you must be sore.'

Iseult shook her head with an effort, not even able to lift it from where it lay on Nadim's shoulder. She sounded drunk. 'No…not sore…happy.'

She only started coming back up through the layers of satedness when she felt Nadim lower her into a warm, fragrant bath and felt the water close over her languid body. His arms were leaving, pulling away, and instinctively she made a sound of protest, catching his arm, finally opening her heavy eyes.

She was in a bathing area much like her own, but far bigger and more opulent. Nadim's arm was under her hand, and she saw that he'd put on a robe. She felt completely disorientated, and if an alien had appeared in that moment with the news that they'd arrived on another planet she wouldn't have been surprised.

Nadim pressed a kiss to her mouth, and a chain reaction started in Iseult's blood. She wanted to ask Nadim to get into the bath with her, but something in his closed expression forbade it. He looked cool and composed, austere again. Not like the man who'd told her with such a tortured expression that he wanted her. And who had then made love to her…had initiated her into womanhood.

She took her hand from his arm, something inside her contracting protectively amongst the feelings of opiate languour.

Nadim stood up and towered over Iseult in the bath. 'I've left a robe on the chair for you. I'll be outside when you're ready…'

Iseult watched him walk out, and felt alternately

as if he'd just slapped her across the face and as if he'd just given her the greatest gift. She sank down in the water, wanting to hide away, feeling hideously self-conscious all of a sudden. Deeply embedded doubts and fears started to rise up to the surface.

Had she initiated this? Had she somehow twisted things again so that she could justify it to herself because Nadim had really wanted her? Had she thrown herself at him like some out-of-control groupie?

Her belly quivered when she remembered how he'd lifted her up and carried her to his tent like a marauding pirate. A tiny trickle of confidence returned. He'd told her he'd wanted her from the moment he'd seen her…so that tension in Ireland hadn't been her imagination…but why was he being so aloof now?

Iseult's brain started to throb with questions and insecurities and attempts to reassure herself. Sitting up to wash herself perfunctorily, she stopped for a moment when she saw faint bruises flowering across her skin, redness from where Nadim's stubble had grazed her delicate skin. Heat bloomed low again, and Iseult avoided touching that part of herself which still tingled and stung slightly.

Nadim stood at the heavily draped curtains at the entrance to his tent. Hard to believe that only an hour or so had passed, when the entire world seemed to have shifted on its axis. Sounds of revelry came faintly from the tent he'd left earlier. But all he could remember was the sheer blind lust that had galvanised him.

When he'd first spotted Iseult in the tent, dressed in that excuse of an outfit, he hadn't recognised her. But he hadn't been able to look away. She'd been more inherently voluptuous than the other girls, and her movements had been gauche and untutored. It had been odd, as the girls who danced that dance would have learnt it from their own mothers at a young age.

His eye had been drawn to the unknown woman and his body had stirred in response. Nadim's first feeling had been intense relief—*Iseult hasn't bewitched me completely*. But almost in the same instant, she'd come closer, and he'd had the sinking realisation that it could be none other than her. The perfect pale alabaster of her skin had glowed with luminescence in the dim light. And her eyes, flashing dark gold above that veil, had given her away completely.

And then had come the burning acrid jealousy because every other man there would be looking at her and coveting her charms. It had taken all his control and self-restraint to wait until she'd disappeared at the back of the tent to go and get her. And the minute he'd pulled her into his body he'd known that there was only one possible outcome to that scenario.

The knowledge sliced through his brain and body as if he'd been blocking it out: *she'd been a virgin*. And yet she'd made love to him with such passionate abandon that if he hadn't felt her body's initial resistance he might not even have known.

He'd only ever slept with one other virgin: his wife. Nadim's brain seized there. Yet another comparison thrown up to mock him and make his belly roil with guilt as he had to acknowledge the vast differences between the two women...

He realised then that the splashing of the bath had stopped, and he heard a soft footfall behind him. Feeling intense trepidation, he slowly turned around to face Iseult.

CHAPTER TEN

ISEULT steeled herself for whatever was coming, even though she had no idea what that might be. She belted the robe around her waist tightly. Between her legs she could feel tenderness, and the memory of how it had felt to have Nadim surge so forcefully into her body made her feel weak with desire all over again.

Slowly he turned around, his face unreadable, his long robe concealing his body. He came into the tent, the drapes falling closed again behind him.

'Why didn't you tell me you were innocent?'

The simple question blindsided Iseult for a moment, but she recovered. 'Would you have slept with me if you'd known?'

No way, was Nadim's quick and instinctive response—along with a rogue voice saying, *Liar, you wouldn't have been able not to.*

As Iseult watched, she could see Nadim battle with something, but eventually he said, 'Probably not, no.'

Iseult ducked her head, ashamed of having been duplicitous on any level, and had to admit, 'I think I knew that…but I didn't want you…not to sleep with me.'

She lifted her chin again, feeling something defiant move through her. She knew if she had the moment again she'd act in the same way. She'd wanted Nadim and he'd wanted her.

Nadim had moved closer and Iseult could feel heat rising. His smell wound round her again, and that musky tang of *sex*.

'You know this changes everything.'

Iseult could only look at Nadim. 'What do you mean?' She had a sudden horrifying vision of Nadim telling her that because he'd been her first lover some ancient desert law decreed that they should be married.

As if reading her mind, he quirked a hard smile and said mockingly, 'You can stop that overactive imagination right there. This may be a country with indelible ties to ancient customs, but those customs don't apply to women I decide to take as my mistresses…'

For a long second his words didn't sink in. *Mistresses*. There was something so inherently insulting about that word and title. As archaic as the laws he'd just spoken of. And yet Iseult had to mock herself. Nadim was hardly the kind of man who'd have something as trite as a *girlfriend* or a *partner.* He was of the modern world and yet *not* of the modern world.

She tried to comprehend. 'You're saying that just because we've slept together now I'm your mistress?'

He moved closer, and Iseult's hands tightened on her belt. Her breath hitched unsteadily. 'Precisely that's what I'm saying. Sleeping with you once is not enough. Not by a long shot. You're innocent, Iseult. I can teach you…help you explore your sensuality.'

Iseult's brain melted, and the part of her that rebelled was drowned out. How could he know what he said? How could he know that with those few words he was taking out one of her innermost vulnerabilities, looking at it in the light and saying, *Let me help you with this.*

She shook her head and felt her hair move across one shoulder, saw how Nadim's eyes flicked there momentarily and how his eyes grew darker. Her heart thumped in response. 'I…don't know how I feel about that.'

In a cataclysmic second he was close enough to snake a hand around her waist and pull her into his body. Their robes were so flimsy she could already feel the potent burgeoning strength of him, and at that moment the thought of being denied another chance to sleep with this man was anathema to Iseult.

His eyes blazed down into hers, mesmeric. 'I'm offering you all I can give, Iseult. You will be my mistress and we will explore this attraction for as long as we both feel it.'

How could she think when he was so close? When it felt as if a mythical kingdom lay just beyond the tent, calling to her seductively to give in? When this man had woken her from a deep dark and cold sleep and shown her an enticing taste of what it was to be a desirable woman? Iseult couldn't believe that there was anything more to this than sheer random carnal attraction. But one thing she did know: if anyone had the ability to make her feel beautiful it was going to be this man, and *now*. Nadim was making it perfectly clear to Iseult this would only last for a very finite time.

Feeling as if she was stepping out over a cliff-edge and into a void of nothing, Iseult just said shakily, 'Okay…'

An expression crossed Nadim's face—one that made Iseult tense instinctively; it had looked like cynicism. She had a sudden flash of understanding that she'd just joined the leagues of other women who'd never said no to him, and for a second wished that she could be stronger. But, feeling her tension, Nadim pulled her even closer, and now his expression was full of only one thing: desire.

Taking Iseult's hand in his, he led her back to the bed, which was still rumpled. He lay down and pulled her down to lie alongside him, the movement causing her gown to slide aside so that one breast was exposed.

Immediately embarrassed, Iseult went to cover up again, but Nadim stopped her hand, pulling the robe further apart and down her arm, making Iseult's pulse throb between her legs when she saw how he looked at her. Her breast flowered under his gaze, swelling and tightening, the tip becoming an aching hard point.

Before he touched her, though, Nadim asked innocuously, 'Are you hungry?'

Iseult's throat dried. She was, but not for food. As if reading her mind, Nadim chuckled darkly and said, 'You are learning fast, my sweet Iseult... time for food later, I think...'

Feeling desperately wanton, Iseult couldn't move as Nadim bent and cupped her breast and brought that tingling peak into his mouth where he sucked hard. Iseult gasped. Her hand tightened on the bedclothes. And then he pushed her back and opened her robe fully, spreading it apart, baring her to his gaze.

With a dark look of intent he started to press kisses down over her flat belly to where dark red curls hid the secret place of her desire. She felt Nadim's hands spread her legs apart and said shakily, through the fire building at her core, 'Nadim?'

He looked up at her, all dark and awe-inspiring, and said, 'This time is going to be all about you and your pleasure. I will show you another way to fall off the edge…'

As Iseult watched he started to press teasing hot kisses up her inner thighs, and then she felt his breath feather between her legs as he showed her exactly what he meant.

The following early evening Iseult looked around at where men were taking down tents, packing up. Lina had already left with Iseult's baggage, and now she waited for Nadim by his Jeep. For their return to Merkazad, there was no question of how she was travelling. She was with Nadim. As effectively as if she had a sign around her neck that proclaimed, *I slept with Nadim and am now his property!*

But even that thought couldn't dampen the ardour in her veins as she saw Nadim in the distance, with his head inclined towards an old and gnarled man who leant on a stick, listening patiently. He'd awoken a hunger within her that she feared might never be quenched.

Even the memory of Lina's reaction to her arrival back at her own tent early that afternoon couldn't quench the heat. The teasing, warmly affectionate banter was gone, and Lina had morphed into someone who wouldn't meet Iseult's eyes.

She'd acted with such an obsequious manner that Iseult had felt a little ill. When she'd asked Lina if something was wrong, Lina had replied evasively that nothing was wrong, but clearly things were different now. Iseult had become part of Nadim's retinue and therefore had to be treated accordingly.

Even so...Iseult couldn't feel regret or remorse for the decision she'd taken. She watched Nadim stride towards her, with his cream robes billowing out around him, and felt weak with longing.

As they made the journey back down the mountains and into the Merkazadi plateau again, Nadim spent most of his time on a cellphone, speaking in a dizzying array of languages. One minute French, the next Spanish, back to English, and then something unmistakably Arabic.

Iseult tried to relax and look at the scenery but it was impossible. Her body seemed to be vibrating at a higher frequency, and Nadim would periodically reach for her hand, touching her, seeking her eyes, setting off a chain reaction of heat waves through her body and over her skin.

Nadim had made love to Iseult over and over again, but each time without seeking his own release. He was letting her body get used to the pleasure he could so effortlessly evoke, and even though she'd begged him to take her he'd held back, showing her how pleasure could come in many different ways. It had left her feeling sated and restless all at the same time.

'What are you thinking of?'

Iseult whirled around, face flushing. She'd been so engrossed that she hadn't even heard him terminate his conversation. 'No…nothing…' she stuttered ineffectually, as she feared what she had been thinking about must be engraved all over her face.

Nadim smiled that seductive, mocking smile and took her hand, taking it to his mouth where he pressed a kiss against her inner palm. Iseult squirmed and blushed and tried to pull her hand away. '*Don't*…the driver…'

She looked to the front, but the driver was looking resolutely forward. Nadim let her hand go and drawled softly, 'We're as good as alone. Asad doesn't speak English.'

Iseult blushed more. 'That may be, but he wouldn't have to speak English to know what's going on.'

A familiarly autocratic look crossed Nadim's face, and Iseult cut in before he could speak. 'I know, I know—you're the Sheikh and no one questions what you do. But what about me? I have to work—'

'You don't have to work any more…'

Iseult's mouth opened and closed. As much as

she hated the thought of gossip, she wasn't going to hide away either. Fire built in her belly and she rounded fully on Nadim. 'I am not going to be locked up in that castle like some concubine. I want to keep working with Devil's Kiss. And I want to help Jamilah in the stables.'

Nadim shrugged, nonchalantly picking a bit of non-existent lint off his regal cuff. 'I have no problem with you working—as long as you're in my bed when I want you…'

He came close then, and Iseult saw that his nonchalance was just a thin veneer. She'd angered him again with her outspokenness. 'You're my mistress now, Iseult, in my bed until I say so…'

Rebellion quivered in Iseult's belly. 'What about me? Don't I have any say in this?'

He shook his head, and again reality chaffed. No other woman had ever questioned his intentions. 'Not really, *habiba.*'

Distracted for a second, Iseult asked, 'What does that mean? *Habiba?*' He'd called her that a few times over the past night.

Nadim's mouth twisted for a moment. Something dark crossed his face, and then with clear reluctance he said, 'It means *beloved*…but it's just a figure of speech.' He put a finger under Iseult's chin, and his voice was hard. 'I know how your first lover can inspire feelings… Don't fall in love with me, Iseult. I *won't* be responsible for your heart.'

The sharp pain that gripped her chest made her lash out without thinking about what she was saying. 'I can take care of myself. I wouldn't be foolish enough to give my heart to someone who didn't even love his own wife.'

Nadim's eyes flashed in angry response and his hand tightened on her chin. Immediately Iseult felt contrite. But before she could say anything he just replied, 'Good. Then we both know where we stand.'

Iseult jerked her chin away from Nadim's finger, going cold inside at the evidence of his implacable stance. 'And, anyway, who's to say you won't fall in love with *me*?'

Something about her was so endearingly vulnerable, like a lion cub standing up to a much bigger opponent, that Nadim had to curb his reflex to haul her into him, crush her against his chest and kiss her into oblivion, until they were both going up in flames and it would be the easiest thing in the world to slip out of his robes and open her jeans and pull them down... He cursed the driver just inches away. He might not understand English, but Iseult was right. He already had a damn good idea what was going on. His whole retinue did after he'd carried Iseult into his tent last night like some ancient warrior.

The lack of his usual control made him say starkly now, 'I won't fall in love, Iseult. You can be assured of that. Love serves no purpose in my life.'

As she looked at him he could see something much more vulnerable cross over her face, and she said quietly, 'But you'll marry again some day…'

'Yes, of course,' he dismissed easily with a hand. 'But this time I'll make sure that my chosen bride is under no illusions that there will be love.' His face was no less harsh, but not as closed as he said, 'The present, Iseult, is all I'm interested in, and *you* are the present. When we get back to Merkazad you'll see that Lina will have moved your things to a room closer to mine.'

Iseult's mouth twisted. 'Out of the women's quarters and into the harem?'

Nadim smiled. 'Something like that.'

Iseult shivered, and wondered what it was about this man—how he could hold her in such thrall when he could be so cold and cruel. She wondered if his aversion to the notion of falling in love had become hardened by the very tragic and weighty expectations of his wife. She could understand that as a ruling monarch the luxury of falling in love wouldn't be an acceptable reason for marriage. He would have to marry strategically and well.

Nadim's phone rang again at that moment and he

answered it curtly, releasing Iseult from his intense gaze. She welcomed the brief respite, but cast him a quick, surreptitious glance and felt weak all over again just looking at his regal profile—that strong jaw, that olive skin—and remembering how he'd so easily brought her to ecstasy countless times with just his hands…his mouth.

Was she being the biggest fool on earth to indulge in such folly? Two voices warred in her head with contradictory answers… She knew that unless she was to walk away completely, and go home and risk the security he now gave her family, she had no choice but to stay. And, if she was being completely honest, she knew she couldn't leave. This man was taking her on a sensual journey and she simply didn't have the will to deny herself. Not when she'd resigned herself to a fate of never exploring it.

Jamilah and Nadim needn't have warned Iseult to be careful; she wouldn't be falling for him. No way.

It was very hard to cling to that assertion, though, some hours after they'd arrived back at the castle and Iseult heard the door of her bedroom open and close quietly. Her new bedroom was even more sumptuous than the last one, but none of that captivated her now. What captivated her was the tall, broad figure that darkened her doorway, long flowing robes barely concealing his powerful physique.

In a few long strides he was by her bed and the robe was gone. Iseult's throat dried at the stunningly perfect musculature of Nadim's body as he stood tall and proud. He reached down and twitched back the sheets. Iseult lay there in just pants and a T-shirt. Nadim grimaced. 'I need to see about getting you some more alluring nightwear.'

Instantly Iseult was defensive, reaching down for the sheet again. But Nadim came down beside her and stopped her hands. She rounded on him. 'I'm not some doll you can just dress up for your pleasure only. I happen to be very comfortable as I am.'

With his hands holding her captive, and far more naked than her, Nadim bent down and covered her mouth with his, kissing her deeply and so thoroughly that by the time he'd finished she was dizzy with lust.

He growled at her, 'You could be dressed in a coarse sack and you'd still turn me on…but you need to know the sensuality of silk and lace too… and I can do that for you…'

Rendered defenceless just by his kiss, Iseult said unthinkingly, 'I don't need silk or lace. I just need you…'

Nadim released her hands and pulled at her

T-shirt until she lifted her arms and it was gone. Sitting back for a moment, he looked his fill at her beautiful full breasts, with their hard rosy tips. She lay back like a courtesan of old, hands above her head, hair spread out around her in glorious abandon, and Nadim had to wonder in that moment if he'd been mistaken—if she hadn't been as innocent as he'd believed.

But just as he thought that she bit her lip and brought her hands down to cover her breasts, and something exultant moved through him. To disguise it, he bent forward and took her hands away, and before lavishing attention on each generous mound of flesh he said, 'And no more unflattering sports bras…'

Iseult sucked in a breath and closed her eyes when she felt Nadim's mouth on her. Hot, wet, and sucking her into some parallel universe of pleasure. With an economy and deftness of movement he'd taken off her knickers, sliding them down her legs, and then he was right beside her, the whole length of his naked body next to hers.

Iseult instinctively closed a hand around him in an intimate caress, loving the feel of his steely strength covered with such silk. 'Please, Nadim…' she said between drugging kisses. 'I want you to make love to me…like you did before.'

Nadim pulled back for a moment. His hand smoothed down over her contracting belly and

sought the juncture of her thighs, where she felt
so wet she was embarrassed. 'You're not tender
any more?'

Iseult was struck at his concern. This was why
he'd held back? She shook her head and moaned
softly when she felt him penetrate her with a
finger, moving her hips towards him in wanton
abandonment.

She barely heard the foil wrapper, or saw him
smooth the protection over his erection. He didn't
lie her flat on her back; he pulled her in close to his
body, face to face. She felt him lift her leg so that
it lay over his hip, opening her to him intimately.

And then he shifted down slightly, and she felt
the blunt head of him at her slick entrance, and
then with a surge of power his mouth found hers
and his body penetrated hers so fully that stars
danced before her eyes.

Her hands were clasped around his neck, hips
locked with his. Nadim was buried inside her, and
in that moment, before he started moving again,
Iseult knew that whatever assurances she'd given
herself earlier about not falling for him were lies,
lies, lies.

Nadim started to move, slowly and powerfully, in and out. His mouth moved down her jaw
and neck and Iseult couldn't think any more. He
cupped her breast, and as he thrust again he took
it into his mouth, sucking roughly, biting gently.

Iseult's hand funnelled into his silky hair, holding him to her as her back arched into him even more, as her leg tightened around his hip, clasping him to her, while his powerful buttocks threatened to make her world explode.

And, feeling one long thrust deep inside her, Iseult couldn't hold back and did explode—and it was far more earth-shattering than anything she'd known before.

When Iseult woke the next morning to the alarm clock on her phone, she knew she was alone in the bed—on her front, spreadeagled in abandon. She immediately felt self-conscious and grabbed for the sheet, pulling it over her and lying on her back.

Her whole body felt sated and lethargic, as if some soporific drug had been injected into her veins. When she and Nadim had recovered last night, after making love *again*, Nadim had cradled her against him as her breath had finally returned to normal after the tumult. But then he'd extricated himself from her embrace, picked up his robe and left the room as quietly as he'd entered.

Iseult had heard the term *wham-bam, thank you, ma'am* before, but never really had a context for it. Now she did.

And yet, she had to ask herself angrily, what had she expected? She could be under no illusions. Nadim had been brutally clear and honest from the

very start. What *had* she expected? Tender words
of love? Hours of cuddling and hand-holding?

Despite the unwelcome realisation that perhaps this was how his wife had felt, Iseult felt her
treacherous heart give a little lurch in longing, and
suddenly she knew with a terrible misgiving that
Nadim had the potential to destroy her.

That evening Iseult ached all over: from tension
and from work. She'd held her head high all day,
but it was clear in the way that everyone treated
her now that they all knew about her new status in
Nadim's life...and bed. People walked on eggshells
around her, and she could only hope and pray that
if she resolutely got on with the job as normal
they'd soon forget about it...

To her intense relief Jamilah had treated her no
differently. She'd given Iseult an enigmatic look,
but then Iseult had noticed that the other woman
had been distracted and slightly strained-looking
herself. When she went looking for her at the end
of the day, to see if anything was wrong, Jamilah
had gone out somewhere.

Taking advantage of Jamilah's empty office,
Iseult called home to speak to her brothers and
sister and father, as it had been a few days. Putting
down the phone on the conversation, she took a
deep breath—just as Jamilah's door opened with
a bang and Nadim stood there, glowering.

Immediately Iseult's protective instincts kicked in, and her back stiffened even as another part of her melted inside to see him dressed in a stunning suit and tie, every inch of him the urbane business-man again.

'Why aren't you up at the castle waiting for me?'

Iseult stood up, quivering from head to toe at his autocratic tone. 'I wasn't aware of any schedule I had to follow—perhaps there's some *Mistress to the Sheikh* guidebook I need to study?'

Nadim came in and closed the door behind him, instantly threatening. 'Still as impudent as ever. So much for hoping that passion might tame that tongue of yours.'

Iseult's shoulders straightened. 'I'm not some animal that can be *tamed*, Sheikh. Just because I've stupidly agreed to sleep with you it does not mean that I've become lobotomised in the process. Strange as this might sound, it wasn't my life's ambition to become the mistress of a sheikh.'

To Iseult's utter surprise, Nadim threw his head back and laughed uproariously. He came even closer, eyes sparkling, and pulled a resisting Iseult into him.

She struggled and said, feeling curiously emo-tional all of a sudden, 'Don't laugh at me.'

Suddenly all mirth was gone as Nadim looked down into her eyes and said, almost musingly, 'I think that's why you're so good with thorough-breds…you can sense their struggle against being tamed and they can sense your empathy…'

It was the first time anyone had articulated what Iseult had always felt instinctively.

And then he said huskily, all arrogance and autocracy gone, 'I thought we'd moved on from Sheikh? And you weren't stupid to agree to sleep with me…I think that was a very wise decision… In any case, you weren't going to be allowed to refuse.'

'I wasn't?' Iseult asked shakily, mesmerised by the tension in his body and his glittering gaze.

Nadim shook his head. 'No. I wouldn't have rested until I had you exactly where I wanted you.'

He pulled at the band holding her hair up in its habitual ponytail and she felt her hair fall down around her shoulders, saw how his eyes followed the movement. He was so close now she could feel the latent strength in his body, could feel him stir against her, and she had to fight not to squirm against him.

He looked down at her again and quirked his mouth. 'I don't think Jamilah would appreciate us making love on her desk, do you?'

Iseult shook her head faintly, a gush of liquid heat rushing to her groin at the sudden image of

Nadim stripping and spreading her back on the desk to move between her legs and take her.

'Well, if we don't make a move soon, that's exactly what's going to happen. We're having dinner together this evening in my rooms, and I've bought you some gifts…'

Nadim watched a wary look cross Iseult's face as he took her hand to lead her from the room. He could still remember the hot irritation that had surged through him at finding she hadn't returned to her rooms. Through all his intensive meetings today he hadn't been able to concentrate—helplessly distracted when images of their night together last night had inserted themselves with dismaying frequency into his mind.

The hunger to see her again had been so powerful that when she hadn't been waiting meekly for him he'd seen red and come racing down to the stables—only to find her in Jamilah's office, evidently calling home.

Iseult let Nadim lead her out of the office and into his Jeep, parked just outside. All the way up to the castle silence hung around them like a cloak.

Once at the entrance to the castle he said, 'Hisham will come for you in an hour…'

She turned to go and he called her back, his face unreadable but his eyes so black she felt breathless. 'I'd like you to wear the gold dress…'

Before she could protest that she didn't have a

gold dress he'd turned to walk away, and it was only when she walked into her room and saw Lina amidst what looked like an explosion of glittering paper and bags and boxes that she recalled what he had said about getting her gifts. Lina's face was uncovered, even though she still wore the veil, and she too seemed to be mesmerised enough to forget her new distance. Her eyes sparkled.

'Look, Miss Iseult! All this for you!'

Iseult felt a little stunned and weak. She sat on the bed, and then had to jump up when she realised she'd sat on a pair of shoes. She picked them up. They were gorgeous. Dark green suede, with diamanté details on one side. Heels so high they looked lethal.

Lina was in officious mode, and had obviously been given instructions. She herded Iseult to the bathroom now, where Iseult saw a full bath, complete with floating rose petals and lighted candles. Iseult resisted, feeling as though she could only tarnish such a seductive picture. Somehow in the desert it had been easier to take—as if she had matched the rugged terrain.

But Lina, for all her petiteness and delicacy, was surprisingly strong, and had Iseult stripped and in the bath before she quite knew how it had happened. Lying in the bath, feeling totally unlike herself, Iseult could hear the rustle of paper outside, and the clang of hangers as Lina hung things up. Every now and then there'd be a silence, and then just a long deep sigh as Lina obviously came across something too beautiful to resist sighing over.

But this was no fairytale. She was the Sheikh of al Saqr's mistress and he was just kitting her out.

If anything Iseult should be feeling insulted… angry… But when she walked back into her bedroom in just a towel, and saw Lina standing at the mirror holding up a vision of a golden dress, anger was all too elusive.

CHAPTER ELEVEN

LINA turned and held out the dress with reverent hands. It was a tunic made in what looked like pure gold, with intricate embroidery around the hem in deep iridescent silver. When Lina brought it closer, the colour shimmered in the light, showing a whole range of different shades of gold running through it.

On the bed lay a couple of wisps of underwear, also gold in colour. Iseult felt sweaty, and fear prickled over her skin. 'Lina, I can't wear this... I'll wear my jeans...'

But Lina whipped the towel off Iseult so fast that she yelped, and had no choice but to get into the underwear if she wanted to cover up. The bra looked minuscule, but it fitted like a glove. The pants were cut like French knickers. Lina handed her a pair of slim-fitting trousers in the same material as the dress and she put them on, followed by the dress.

It whispered down over her body and hips, cut

with a daringly low V-neck, so that a tiny hint of lace from the bra could be seen in her shadowy cleavage.

'It's pure Indian silk, Miss Iseult.'

Lina sat her down and started to dry her hair, taking it back on one side and holding it in place with an ornate, antique-looking comb, leaving the rest to fall over her shoulder. Then she put some kohl on her eyes, and mascara, making Iseult look almost as mysterious as the women she'd seen in the streets that day she'd gone out with Jamilah to buy clothes. After a moment Lina stood back to admire her handiwork and said, 'You are lovely, Miss Iseult.'

Iseult grimaced at her reflection. The truth was she almost didn't recognise herself, and this whole experience was so close to a dream she'd buried deep within her that she wasn't sure if she could stand without trembling all over.

Lina had disappeared, and now returned holding out a pair of kitten-heeled gold sandals. Iseult got up shakily and put them on, all fingers and thumbs on the delicate clasps until Lina bent down to help her.

Just then there was a knock on the outer door and Lina said, 'That'll be Hisham. He'll escort you to Sheikh Nadim's rooms.'

Iseult's cheeks burned. Did absolutely everyone know what was going on? Lina all but pushed her out through the door, and Iseult followed the slightly wizened man who led the way.

By the time they'd reached Nadim's room, which they'd climbed up another level to reach, Iseult's heart was thumping and she was dry-mouthed with fear. All she could imagine was that either Nadim wouldn't be there—it had all been some huge mistake—or that he'd take one look and laugh at her efforts to try and be...beautiful.

But Hisham was knocking, and the door was opening, and...there was Nadim. All Iseult's doubts fled in a flood of heat. He was dressed formally in a white shirt and black trousers, shirt open at the neck. He'd obviously not long showered, as his hair was still damp and curling slightly.

He said something indecipherable to Hisham, who melted away, and then he was reaching out a hand for Iseult and drawing her into his rooms. With her hand in his, she could only gape at the sheer magnificence of his suite. Gold and cream brocade, abundant fresh flowers...doors open and leading out onto a private patio that overlooked the entire complex, and the lights of Merkazad glittering in the distance against the dusky sky.

He let her go briefly, but Iseult hardly noticed she was so mesmerised by the view. Eventually she turned around and saw Nadim pouring a honey-coloured sparkling drink into two crystal glasses. She walked back in and Nadim handed her a glass. 'A toast,' he said.

Iseult held her glass up to his and Nadim said throatily, 'To you, Iseult. You are beautiful tonight.'

Immediately, despite his words, Iseult felt self-conscious and awkward. She blushed and took a sip of the sparkling liquid, nearly coughing when the bubbles fizzed effervescently down her throat. Nadim smiled and quirked a brow. 'Have you had champagne before?'

A little of Iseult's fire returned. 'Of course. I'm not a complete hick.' She smiled then too. 'But I'd wager that the champagne I've tasted isn't exactly of the same vintage as this.'

Nadim was transfixed by the smile curving Iseult's generous mouth. In truth he'd been transfixed since he'd seen her at his door with Hisham. He'd expected her to be lovely in the gold dress he'd picked out…but she was so much more than that. The material skimmed her curves, clung to the lush line of her breasts, her small waist, the surprisingly womanly flare of her hips.

Her hair shone like a glowing red flame against the gold and, just as he'd suspected they would, her eyes looked even tawnier. She walked away now, to look at something, and Nadim heard her ask, 'Is this your wife?'

Iseult knew she shouldn't have asked as soon as

the words came out of her mouth and tension came into the room. She looked from the framed picture to Nadim warily, and then back again. The dark woman was incredibly pretty, and she was gazing up at a younger, softer-looking Nadim so adoringly that Iseult felt a physical pain pierce her heart.

'Yes,' he said briefly, curtly. 'That's Sara. I'm sorry. I should have put it away.'

Iseult disguised the dart of hurt. Despite everything he'd said, he had to have had *some* feelings for his wife—or else why would he keep such a memento close by? She turned away from it and said, 'Don't be ridiculous, Nadim, she was your wife. It'd be strange if you didn't have pictures around.'

He looked incredibly harsh in the luxuriant gold light of the many dim lamps, but he just said, 'The only ridiculous thing is how far away you are from me. Come over here.'

Iseult firmly shut the door on the pain that seeing the picture of his wife had engendered and walked over, saying lightly, 'You're so bossy. Has anyone ever told you that?'

He smiled then, a genuine smile, as if something had relaxed inside him, and reached for her hand as soon as she was close enough. 'No. Only you have the sheer audacity to insult the Sheikh of Merkazad.'

'Good thing, too, I'd say. It must be unbearable with all that bowing and scraping going on.'

They smiled at each other, and Iseult felt an alien lightness unfurling inside her. Just then a discreet knock sounded at the door, and Nadim emitted a brief instruction in Arabic.

In an instant the room seemed to be full of a stream of staff, entering carrying steaming plates of the most mouthwatering food. Nadim led her back out to the terrace, where a table had been set with candles flickering gently in the warm breeze.

With speed and economy of movement, plates and platters were laid out, and Hisham stood patiently by, asking if they needed anything else.

Nadim shook his head, and as the man turned to go Iseult said, *'Shukran.'*

When he'd left she turned to Nadim and saw the expression on his face. 'What?' she asked nervously.

'You've been learning Arabic?'

Iseult shrugged, feeling self-conscious again. 'Jamilah has been teaching me a few words.'

It was crazy for Nadim to feel suddenly jealous of Jamilah teaching Iseult Arabic, but he did. Feeling uncharacteristically out of control, he pulled out a chair for Iseult to sit down. When she moved her scent wrapped around him like a caress. He sat down opposite Iseult and poured them both some wine. He held up his glass, 'Well, if you'll permit me, perhaps this evening I can teach you a little about traditional Merkazadi food…'

A couple of hours later Iseult protested, putting up a hand. 'Please, no more food. I've never eaten so much in my life.'

Nadim reluctantly put down a plump and succulent date. Watching Iseult taste and eat the array of dishes and then feast on the dates had him so tightly wound that he had to exert some control over his rogue hormones.

Iseult sat back and let a delicious languour invade her veins. She'd never thought eating dinner had erotic possibilities, but she knew after sharing dinner with Nadim this evening she'd never sit at another table with him and not blush.

He'd dismissed the use of knives and forks and had fed her himself. Balls of mashed rice infused with delicate spices. Morsels of Kingfish that broke apart on his fingers so she had to stick out her tongue to catch them. Wine…and dates…fat dates…oozing with illicit sticky sweetness, washed down with strong, tart coffee called *khawa*.

He sat back and looked at her for a long moment, and then said, 'I thought you were too thin when I first met you.'

Iseult attempted humour to deflect the intensity

that seemed to drench the air around them. 'So you're just trying to fatten me up?'

He sat forward. 'It must have been hard for you, covering for your father and trying to keep things going.'

Iseult blinked, shocked out of the languid desire that had been sneaking through her veins. Instant shame came back—the shame of her father's illness that they'd all done their best to cover up. Iseult's mouth twisted, and she played with her empty coffee cup. 'It wasn't that bad really…'

Nadim caught her eye and raised a brow. 'I know how hard Jamilah works, and she has a whole team under her. I know how hard it is to run even moderate-sized stables. And then to have to deal with an alcoholic parent…'

Iseult was defensive. 'My father never got abusive or angry. He just…tried to drown his sorrows—literally.' Iseult shrugged minutely and looked out to the glittering view of Merkazad in the far distance, with the distinctive minaret of the mosque standing out. 'As for keeping things going…I never really had time to think about it.'

That bare explanation hid the sheer toil she'd endured on a daily basis, sometimes skipping school to work at home. Saying anything that might be construed as wanting sympathy had always been anathema to her.

Wanting to divert Nadim's intense regard, she

remembered something he'd said in Ireland. She looked back at him. 'What did you mean when you said you knew what it was like to have everything you know jeopardised?'

Nadim was quiet for a long moment, and then stood from his chair, taking his glass of wine with him, and went to stand against the stone balustrade of the private balcony.

He spoke so quietly at first that Iseult had to strain to hear, and then silently she got up too and went to stand with her back to the view, just looking at Nadim's proud profile.

'It happened a couple of times. We'd always had an uneasy alliance with Al-Omar. We'd been gifted our independence many years before, but when the current Sultan's great-grandfather took control he wanted Merkazad back under his control. He never managed to attack, but the intention went down the line. When I was twelve we were attacked by the Sultan's father and taken by surprise as we hadn't had to defend ourselves for many years...'

Iseult was mesmerised, leaning on one elbow to listen. What Nadim spoke of was utterly fantastical.

'Salman and I were woken in the middle of the night by my mother and told to get out of bed and sneak down through secret passages, but we were caught.'

'What happened?'

'We were held prisoner in an ancient jail in the basement of the castle.'

Iseult gasped. 'But you were the ruling family. Isn't there some sort of protocol for that?'

Nadim's mouth twisted. He flicked her a glance. 'Not in this world.'

Shakily Iseult asked, 'How long were you kept prisoner for?'

Almost carelessly Nadim said, 'Nearly three months. I think it affected my brother much more profoundly. For some reason our captors used to delight in tormenting him. They would take him out of the jail for hours on end, and when they returned him he wouldn't say a word. I tried to make them take me…but they'd just beat me back.'

He continued briskly, 'We were lucky. Our Bedu neighbours came to help us. Our invaders had grown complacent, thinking that we would just rot away in the dungeon…but we had powerful friends who were more interested in keeping us a sovereign state. And my father was a well-loved ruler. They attacked one night and we were freed. But everything was gone…the stables and stud were ransacked…they'd shot all the horses. The castle was looted of all but the murals on the walls…'

Iseult shook her head, trying to understand how it must have felt, first of all to be incarcerated and then to come out to find everything changed or gone.

He turned to face her, twirling the glass of wine between his long fingers. 'And then my parents died in a plane crash when I was sixteen and Salman twelve. Instantly we were under threat again, but this time we were more prepared as my father had enlisted warriors to keep watch over every strategic weak point in the border, so the ruler of Al-Omar couldn't attack again.'

'The Sultan's father died while I was in school in England, with Salman, and for the first time we knew we might be safe. Advisors ran the country while I finished my education, until I reached the age of twenty-one and could legally take over as Sheikh and ruler...'

Iseult realised something then. 'Jamilah must have been so young when her parents died.'

'Yes, she was only six. She stayed here and went to school in Merkazad. I made sure she was cared for by members of our extended family.'

'But now there's peace? You said that you're friends with the current Sultan?'

Nadim nodded. 'We went to school together in England.' He smiled. 'At first we hated each other, and used to get into fights at every opportunity. But then we discovered a mutual interest in peace and living in a democratic and progressive society and were bonded by our ideals. After his father

died we vowed to forge an iron-clad alliance that
would stand for many generations to come…'

Hearing this made Iseult feel humbled. From
such an early age he'd been aware of responsibility and duty. In many ways they were similar,
and yet…*not*. Iseult's responsibilities had been
confined to a much narrower world. And when
she thought of that she was reminded of the great
yawning chasm between Nadim's life and hers.
Some day he would find a suitable bride and marry
again, go on to have heirs to continue his legacy,
and she— Her mind halted when Nadim put down
his wine glass on the table and reached for her.

As if pulled by a magnet stronger than she could
resist, she went into his arms and shook with emotion—emotion that he was effortlessly arousing.

Nadim trailed a finger down the silky smoothness
of Iseult's cheek. He felt slightly shell shocked.
He'd just blithely spilled his entire life's secrets
to a woman when he'd never felt the desire to do
so before. Lovers had tried to get him to tell what
they thought were fantastic exotic tales, but he'd
seen the manipulative glitter in their eyes, as if
they'd thought it would inspire more intimacy.

The only other woman who had known everything had been his wife, Sara. And that was because she'd come from here and had lived through
everything they had as the daughter of one of his
father's closest allies. He felt bitterness rise when

he thought of it; it was one of the reasons she'd been deemed so *perfect* for him.

But Iseult… What was it about this woman and the effortless feeling of kinship she evoked within him? She was looking down…away. And he jealously wanted her eyes on him… He tipped up her chin with a finger and felt her clench her jaw slightly. What he saw in her eyes was something serious and deep. It sent tendrils of trepidation through him, even amidst a heady sweet feeling he'd never experienced before.

To drive away the regret that he'd said anything at all, and the fleeting panic because he recognised the look in her eyes, he bent his head and kissed her soft mouth, willing passion to come and obliterate any intellectual thought.

Hours later—her beautiful golden dress, underwear and hair-comb long gone—Iseult lay sprawled in inelegant abandon over Nadim's equally naked body. She was pressing little kisses over his chest. His skin was still dewed with moisture and it tasted tangy and musky.

Within seconds of Nadim kissing her out on the balcony everything had been forgotten as intense desire had taken over, obliterating anything but sating their physical needs. She had a strong suspicion that he regretted telling her all he had, but she was too lethargic right now to let that thought bother her.

Iseult put her cheek onto Nadim's chest and felt his heart beating, strong and steadily. She'd never felt so deeply sated in all her life, as if she was drunk and yet never more sober…a heady mix.

Idly, she trailed her hand across Nadim's chest, and then lifted her head and propped her chin on her hand. His eyes were like two dark pools, making her heart kick all over again and fresh tendrils of desire coil through her.

'Do you know,' she mused, 'I've seen you in jeans and a T-shirt…and a suit and tie…and your traditional robes…' She smiled and started to trail her free hand down Nadim's chest, and lower, watching how his eyes darkened even more.

'But I think I like you naked best of all…' Her hand wrapped around him in an intimate caress, and she exulted when she felt him harden and swell under her touch.

He brought his hands to her arms and with an easy strength flipped them, so that Iseult was under him. He hovered over her and between her legs, where his hair-roughened thighs made her move her hips.

In an unconsciously sensual move Iseult bent one leg and ran her foot down the back of Nadim's leg, the soft silky skin of her inner thigh against his hip.

With a growl, he caught that leg and held it. He bent his head to hers and said, 'Remember what I said, Iseult…don't fall in love with me.'

Iseult tried to stem the instant gush of pain, and in that second knew that it was already too late. Somewhere it had happened; it could have even been just now out on the balcony, when he'd told her so dispassionately about his turbulent history, or it could have been in that tent in the desert when he'd first made love to her, or it could have been that moment she'd first seen him in Ireland, but somewhere along the way she'd fallen irrevocably in love.

She knew she couldn't deny it, and that vulnerability made her say defiantly, 'As long as you don't fall in love with me.'

He smiled, and to Iseult's eyes in that moment he looked incredibly sad. He didn't need to say it, but it was written all over his face: *I won't.* And then his mouth met hers, and she twined her hands around his neck, feeling alternately angry with him and absurdly tender, and irritated that all he had to do was kiss her to scramble any rational thought.

CHAPTER TWELVE

'I'D LIKE you to come to the Sultan of Al-Omar's birthday celebrations with me.'

Iseult just looked at Nadim. He was leaning nonchalantly against the door of Devil's Kiss's stable, looking far too gorgeous for his own good in faded jeans and a T-shirt. Earlier she'd watched him break in a new yearling, and it had been sheer poetry in motion.

She stood now, keeping a hand on Devil's Kiss, as if he could keep her rooted in reality. The thought of leaving the cocoon of Merkazad was slightly threatening. 'But…where is it? When?'

Nadim hid the dart of irritation that she wasn't more enthralled at the prospect. 'It starts tomorrow night in B'harani, for family and close friends, and then the main celebration is on Saturday night, when the *crème de la crème* of world society will come to fawn and ogle, and women will vie with one another for the Sultan's favour.'

Iseult felt an equal mix of horror at the thought

of such an event and a wild surge of excitement. She gave a little wry smile, hiding her trepidation. 'Do I have a choice?'

Nadim smiled too, and it was the smile of a wolf. 'Of course not. I was merely allowing you the illusion of choice. If you say no then I'll instruct Lina to do whatever is necessary to render you helpless, and merely carry you there over my shoulder.'

A warm pool of desire settled in Iseult's belly. A little breathlessly she said, 'Well, in that case, I'd love to join you...'

But then she bit her lip as all joking fled and old insecurities rose. It was one thing dressing up for Nadim in his own private rooms, but another thing entirely in public. 'But, Nadim...I'm not... I've never been to anything fancier than a family wedding. I won't know what to do or say...'

'Nonsense,' Nadim declared arrogantly. 'You'll be with me. That's all you need to worry about.'

But the following evening it felt as if Iseult had a lot to worry about. Lina had travelled ahead to B'harani with some of Nadim's retinue early that afternoon, and now she and Nadim were getting into a helicopter which was going to fly them to the same airfield in Al-Omar that she'd flown into just a few weeks before.

Feeling more and more apprehensive and tense, Iseult was silent for the journey, taking in the mountainous landscape below them, looking when Nadim pointed out various things. At the airfield a small private plane was waiting, and the disparity between how she'd flown in and her position now didn't escape her, highlighting the impossible chasm between Nadim's world and hers, and also the tenuous nature of their relationship. Just when would he lose interest? After this weekend? In a week? A month?

After they'd boarded, and were sitting in plush seats, Nadim opened a laptop and became engrossed in whatever he was doing, so Iseult just looked out of the window, glad he wasn't scrambling her brain. The flight was a relatively short thirty minutes, and she sucked in a deep breath when she saw the intricate glittering web of B'harani laid out below as they came in to land. She could make out soaring skyscrapers which glinted in the setting sun, and she could see the Arabian ocean in the distance, like a flat sheet of dark blue.

She turned to Nadim, who had put the laptop away and was watching her. 'I didn't realise B'harani was so big…it's a proper city.'

She winced inwardly, hating that she sounded so gauche. But Nadim just nodded. 'Yes, it's got a population of nearly a million. It's a thriving metropolis. Tourism is a huge industry here for the

Sultan, along with the oil fields out in the desert…
He too has stables and runs a stud.'

Iseult smiled. 'Ah…competition?'

Nadim looked comically affronted. 'No competition at all. He knows who the superior horseman is.'

Iseult thought privately that from what she'd seen very few horse-breeders and trainers would be superior to Nadim.

Just then the plane touched down with a minute bump and they landed.

On disembarking, Iseult saw three limos waiting, all with tinted windows. The air was hot, acrid, and she could taste the salt from the sea. Dusk was turning the sky a bruised colour, and the skyscrapers in the distance made her feel as if she'd travelled to another planet. Merkazad was a world away. But Iseult had a feeling that this place wouldn't lay claim to her the same way that Merkazad had from the moment she'd seen it.

After speeding along a sleek highway that cut right through the towering skyscrapers they turned a corner and drove up what looked like a private road. Right in the centre of the city, a huge, imposing fortress loomed from behind giant walls. It was stunning, soaring and breathtaking.

Nadim said, 'This is the Hussein Palace. Sultan Sadiq's ancestral home.'

Iseult looked at him aghast. 'We're staying here?'

Nadim nodded, obviously amused by Iseult's awe. She made a face at him and looked out of the window again, to see that they were driving into a huge courtyard where what seemed like hundreds of staff in pristine white uniforms waited to greet them.

Nadim was dressed formally in his robes, and Lina had left out a smart trouser suit for Iseult that morning. She was grateful now, as a flurry of activity burst around them and they were summarily ushered into the entrance of the palace.

A huge archway dominated the entrance, and then staff were leading Nadim and Iseult further into the stunning complex, through another open-air courtyard and into a blissfully cool atrium with more soaring ceilings.

Iseult gasped with delight when she saw a multi-coloured bird fly in and out again. One of the staff, a smiling girl who wore a long white *abeyya* but no veil, stopped outside a door and indicated for Iseult to enter.

Nadim sent her a look, and she saw that he was being shown through another door just down the hall. Iseult went in and her eyes widened. The opulence she'd grown used to at Nadim's castle should have inured her to luxury, but it hadn't.

The room was massive, dressed in cool, peaceful

whites. There was an enormous four-poster bed, and a bathroom with a marble sunken bath which looked big enough for a rugby team. Floor-to-ceiling French doors led out to a private garden, complete with lush grass and blooming trees. She heard a door open and saw Nadim step out just a few feet away.

'It's a double suite…our rooms are adjoining.'

'Oh…' Iseult said faintly, the stunning surroundings paling into insignificance as she took in Nadim, his skin so exotically dark against the cream of his robes.

He arched a brow. 'I think a bath before dinner would be nice.'

Iseult said immediately, 'I showered just before we left…' Then she saw the look in his eye and remembered the huge bath and blushed. 'Oh…'

Nadim held out a hand. 'Yes, *oh*. Come here, Iseult…'

A couple of hours later Iseult blushed again in the mirror, as Lina did up her dress at the back, just thinking about what had taken place in Nadim's bath. She'd barely made it out in time to come and meet Lina in her room, and she blushed even harder now, when Lina said, 'You're so flushed, Miss Iseult. Is it the heat?'

Iseult made some strangled reply and meekly followed Lina away from the mirror to sit down, so she could do her hair. After what seemed like an age of pulling and curling, with something that looked like an instrument of torture, Lina stood back and gestured for Iseult to look in the mirror.

Immediate fear gripped Iseult's insides as she approached the reflective glass as if she were walking the plank. *How* had she forgotten this for a moment? How could she be putting herself back in this position again? To be publicly humiliated? Because no matter what Lina had done, no matter how expensive the dress was, she was still tomboy Iseult O'Sullivan from a farm in Ireland.

She stopped in front of the mirror and for a moment couldn't look. And then she did. For a wild moment she didn't recognise the girl in front of her. She wore a long, fitted satin strapless dress in a dark greeny-blue, with an ostrich feather detail over one shoulder. Her skin looked very white, and her breasts swelled enticingly over the bodice. Long glittering green earrings swung against her neck, and Lina had somehow curled her impossibly straight hair and lifted it up and away into a loose chignon. Amidst the glossy red waves a diamanté comb sparkled.

Iseult felt tears burn the back of her eyes, a lump tighten her throat. Just then a knock came to the interconnecting door, and before Iseult could compose herself Nadim strolled in with proprietorial ease.

In an instant he'd politely dismissed Lina, and all Iseult could do was look at him through the mirror. He came to stand behind her, stunning in a black tuxedo. His jaw was tight, and she saw a muscle clench.

He noticed the sheen in her eyes and turned her around, frowning. 'What's wrong?'

Iseult shook her head and looked down, desperately trying to stem the flood of incipient tears, mortified. 'No…nothing…I just—I don't think I can do this. I'm not made for this kind of thing.'

He tipped up her chin. 'You're made for me, Iseult, and you will walk by my side. You are beautiful…do you not see how beautiful you are?'

'I'm not beautiful. Really, I'm not. We'll go into that room and you'll see…and you'll be embarrassed.'

Nadim thought cynically for a moment that Iseult was just fishing for a compliment, but then he saw the genuine distress in her eyes. The genuine disbelief. He shook his head. 'Someone has obviously made you feel that you aren't beautiful. Who was it? Your father?'

Iseult shook her head fiercely. 'No. It was just…' She sucked in a shuddering breath and tried to regain control, sure he wouldn't want to hear of her schoolgirl humiliation. 'I've never been the girly type. I'm not used to this. I'm more at home in a stables or in a field…'

Nadim turned Iseult back to face the mirror, and with his hands on her shoulders bent his head and pressed a heart-meltingly sweet kiss to her cheek. 'You can't hide in the stables for ever,' he said. 'You are beautiful…stunning.' He kissed her jaw. 'Here…' Then he kissed where her neck met her shoulder. 'And here…and everywhere. You will be the envy of every other woman.'

His eyes compelled hers to his in the mirror, until a very fledgling feeling started to burgeon within her—a feeling that felt scarily like *belief*. Nadim turned her around again and said, 'I have something for you.'

He handed her an ornate red box with gold edging. Iseult opened it to reveal a pure gold bottle nestled in white velvet. She looked up at Nadim. 'What is it?'

He quirked a smile. 'Al-Omar is famous for its perfume. It's one I had specially commissioned for you.'

Iseult's heart clenched at the sheer seduction of Nadim, and she wished he wasn't charming her so easily. If he was more perfunctory she could cope; she could pack ice around her heart.

She put the box down with a shaking hand and opened the bottle, taking a tentative sniff before spraying a tiny bit on her wrist. It smelled like an intoxicating mix of delicate roses, together with musk and a hint of tantalising spices.

And as if reading her mind, Nadim said dryly, 'I think it captures your personality. There's amber in there too, because it reminded me of your eyes...'

Speechless, Iseult let Nadim take the bottle out of her hand and spray a tiny bit on her neck, before rubbing it in with a finger. Then he held out her arm and found the delicate skin at her inner elbow and rubbed there. Then he sprayed another bit just above her cleavage. By the time he was finished Iseult was breathing unevenly and her legs were weak.

Nadim put down the perfume and took her hand to lead her out. At the door Iseult stopped him and said huskily, 'Thank you for the perfume... You didn't have to get me anything, but I love it...'

Nadim fought not to let the artlessness of her words grip him tight, like a vice. It only reminded him again of how different she was from other women, and of what a risk he was taking with her. But even so...he knew he couldn't stop.

He just tugged her along and said, 'We'll be late for dinner.'

A couple of hours later Iseult was still in awe of the splendour around them. So much for a gathering for close family and friends. She smiled wryly. There had to be at least two hundred people there, and one or two A-list actors even she recognised.

She'd met Sultan Sadiq Ibn Kamal Hussein before dinner. He was a man cut from the same cloth as Nadim. Tall, handsome and powerfully built. He was also dressed in a tuxedo, and his unusual light blue eyes stood out. He wore an air of jaded cynicism, though, and his forbidding looks to approaching women made Iseult feel sorry for them.

When he'd bent low and taken her hand to press a kiss to the back of it Nadim had pulled her close with a possessive arm that had sent a thrill through her. She'd had to tell herself not to read anything into it. Nadim was no different from this man in many ways.

She saw the tall, debonair Sultan in the distance now, surrounded by a fawning crowd, and wondered if he too had a mistress.

Just then Iseult noticed someone else approaching them, and exclaimed happily, 'Jamilah!' She looked at Nadim. 'I didn't know Jamilah would be here. We could have come together.'

Nadim frowned and said, 'I didn't know she was planning on coming...'

They embraced when Jamilah reached them; she looked even more stunning than usual in a dark royal blue dress that fell in a swirl of silk from just above her bust. Her glossy black hair was tied up in an elaborate chignon, but her face was pale and strained-looking.

Instantly Iseult felt concerned. 'Jamilah, what is it?'

Jamilah smiled tightly. 'Nothing at all.'

But as Iseult watched Jamilah saw something or someone behind them, and went even more pale. Iseult turned around and saw a very tall, strikingly handsome man approaching. A jolt of recognition went through her, even though she'd never seen him before in her life.

She sensed Nadim tense beside her too, and when the other man arrived—so like Nadim in many ways but so different—Nadim said, 'Iseult, I'd like you to meet my brother Salman...'

Iseult shook his hand, but even she could see that he wasn't interested in her or Nadim. He had eyes only for Jamilah, who muttered something about finding someone and fled across the room. Salman watched her go, and Iseult thought she'd never seen anyone look so haunted in all her life. She'd heard gossip around the stables that he was known internationally as the Playboy Sheikh, and rarely came home, but now she could only think of what he and Nadim had been through as young boys.

With the bare minimum of conversation Salman went to leave too, but Nadim stopped him for a moment and said fiercely, 'Don't you think you should leave her alone?'

Salman looked at Nadim, his dark eyes flashing

a warning that Iseult knew well as she'd seen it before. 'Stay out of this, Nadim.'

And then he was gone. Iseult took a deep breath and felt shaky all of a sudden. For a moment there she'd had a vision of how she was going to be reacting in the future, when Nadim had dumped her for his next mistress, or even a wife. At the thought of not being able to be a part of that, she felt a physical pain grip her belly.

Iseult's melancholic mood after witnessing Nadim's exchange with his brother and Jamilah's obvious distress had lingered through the rest of the evening and into the night, even when Nadim had made love to her with an almost fierce abandon, taking them both to a level of ecstasy that had left her shattered.

That melancholy rose again now, as she stood at the wall of the garden outside their rooms and looked out over the stunning city of B'harani in the distance, just beyond the huge walls of the palace.

But all she could see ahead of her was inevitable self-destruction if she continued on this path with Nadim.

She was also very afraid that the longer she indulged herself in this fairytale world of beautiful clothes and a personal maid and being made over on a daily basis, the more deluded she would become in thinking she *was* that kind of person.

Iseult knew herself well enough to believe that while she was sensible enough not to get sucked into that world immediately, it would be headier and more seductive than even she might be able to resist if it went on for much longer. And the mere thought of seeing Nadim take another mistress, or even a wife, nearly made her double over with pain.

A sound came from behind her, and she had a split second of composing herself before she felt a naked body at her back and strong, familiar arms snake around her waist. Iseult closed her eyes and leant back into Nadim, a sudden lump tightening her throat despite her best efforts.

Luckily he couldn't see her face, and when he started to kiss the sensitive back of her neck and said huskily, 'Come back to bed…' Iseult let him take her by the hand and lead her inside. Weakly she told herself that she would give herself this weekend here in B'harani to indulge every aspect of this fairytale moment in time, but that as soon as they were back in Merkazad she had to end this affair.

CHAPTER THIRTEEN

'WE NEED to talk.'

The four words guaranteed to strike fear into the hearts of men everywhere and make them feel weak at the knees—for all the wrong reasons.

Iseult was looking at herself in her bathroom mirror. She tried again. 'Look, Nadim, we need to talk…about *us*.'

She winced and made a face at her reflection. No matter how she said it, it still sounded like dialogue from a bad daytime soap opera.

Just then Lina appeared behind her, and Iseult started.

'Sheikh Nadim is waiting for you.'

Iseult ignored Lina's expressive look at her clothes, and took a deep breath and turned around. She made her way from her room up to Nadim's palatial suite. He was expecting her for dinner. They'd returned from B'harani the day before yesterday, and this was the first moment she would have alone with him since their return.

The second night of Sultan Sadiq's festivities had been as lavish and decadent as Nadim had said it would be. Lina had dressed Iseult in another full-length couture gown, this time in a deep red. And Nadim had presented her with a stunning set of ruby necklace and earrings to wear with it, not listening to her protests for a second. Weakly, Iseult had given herself up to the headiness of it all, guiltily relishing her finite time.

There had been close to a thousand guests, and a world-famous iconic rock band who, despite being in their twilight years, had strutted their stuff like men half their ages. Women on stilts in dresses made entirely of fresh flowers had moved among the guests. Enormous and intricate ice fountains had melted as the evening wore on into pools full of rare multi-coloured fish. Trays of vintage champagne had abounded, and belly dancers had flitted through the guests like exotic birds of prey, reminding Iseult hotly of her own brief foray into that world, and what had happened...

There had also been a charity auction in aid of hundreds of different charities, which had precipitated a spending frenzy that had escalated into the millions. Nadim had contributed some of the most exorbitant sums, clearly in league with Sadiq to up the ante by encouraging competition among the wealthy who hadn't seemed to know when to stop.

He had confided dryly to Iseult at one stage, 'Sadiq likes to lull his monied guests into a false sense of security by putting on a lavish show and then doing his darnedest to extract as much out of them as possible. When they leave after the weekend they're invariably stumped as to how he managed to get them to part with so much money *again*.'

Iseult had tried to sound upbeat, even though with each passing moment she'd grown more melancholic. 'A regular modern-day Robin Hood, with you as his wing man...'

Nadim had shrugged negligently. 'It's not many people in this world who can command a crowd full of some of the most powerful titans of industry, and Sadiq makes the most of it.' He'd winked at Iseult. '*With* a little help from me.'

Iseult was nearing Nadim's door now, and her mind emptied. As much as she knew it would be easy enough to indulge in another night of the dream...perhaps even another couple of weeks... she knew she couldn't. She had to take responsibility for her actions.

Her stomach churning, she knocked lightly and then went in, having a flash of *déjà vu* to when she'd gone into the study at home to have her first discussion with Nadim.

He looked up, smiling, when she walked in, but his smile quickly faded when he saw that she hadn't changed out of her jeans and shirt—the clothes she'd been working in. She closed the door behind her, but didn't move into the room.

He frowned. 'Why haven't you changed?'

Iseult welcomed his censorial tone, allowing her hackles to rise. 'So as your mistress I have to dress to a code? I can't just come up here and be comfortable in jeans?'

Iseult saw how Nadim's body tensed. His eyes narrowed on her. 'What's going on, Iseult?'

Iseult bit her lip and then dived in. 'What's going on is that this affair is over.' She finished in a rush, 'I don't want to be your mistress any more.'

For a long moment Nadim said nothing, and Iseult wondered if she'd imagined saying the words. But then she saw that dangerous look come into Nadim's eyes, and how he literally seemed to shut himself away. Her heart broke. It was starting already.

He put his hands in his pockets and rocked back on his heels. 'What's this about, Iseult? You want more? You want to extract some kind of commitment? You saw something at the weekend and you want a slice of that world permanently? I thought you were different, but perhaps I was naïve to think you wouldn't be swayed by what you've seen.'

Iseult felt sick at his obvious cynicism, and raised a hand in a slashing movement. '*No*. How can you think that?'

Nadim said almost musingly, 'I don't know, Iseult, it's a very seductive world. Are you telling me that out of all the women there last weekend you're the only one who could walk away from it all and *not* want it?'

His voice turned slightly sneering now. 'Or perhaps I've got it wrong. Perhaps you fancy your chances with Sultan Sadiq? I can assure you that we're quite matched when it comes to our fortunes...'

Before Iseult could answer the door opened abruptly, jostling her forward. It was staff arriving with dinner. One look from Nadim made them all melt away instantly.

He looked at her again, dark eyes spearing right through her. 'So is that it? You want more?'

I want you! Iseult wanted to shout, but didn't. Instead she said, 'I want to go home, Nadim. I don't want to see you any more.' For a split second Iseult thought she might bluff her way out of this—confirm his cynicism and protect herself in the process. Her mouth twisted. 'You see, you are partly right. I'm afraid that I'm going to get too used to all of this.' She looked around the room and gestured with a hand. 'And then one day, when you've grown weary of me, I'll be sent back to the stables.'

But then she looked back at him, and knew she couldn't bluff her way out of this by pretending to have grown spoilt. The look of haughty cynicism on Nadim's face was too much to bear.

Defeat laced her voice as she said, 'But it's not the trappings that concern me, Nadim. I've enjoyed every minute of it, but none of it matters really. I'm afraid that it's *you* I want, and you I know I can't have.'

Nadim frowned and tried to understand. He wanted to command Iseult to come closer. She stood near the door in those dusty jeans and shirt, looking as if she was about to bolt like a skittish horse. But he couldn't. Something held him back— some instinct.

'You're my mistress. You have my undivided attention.' He couldn't stop his voice sounding harsh, curt.

Iseult's body flinched slightly, and she hugged her arms around her belly in a classic unconscious gesture of defence. 'For now. But what happens when you lose interest? Obviously you've thought this through, and you'll be able to deal with seeing me every day while you take a new mistress. But I won't be able to deal with that.'

Nadim was growing impatient now. He put out a hand, silently instructing Iseult to come to him, even though an ominous sense of foreboding warned him to be careful. 'You're thinking about something in the future, Iseult. I've no plans to end this any time soon. Come here.'

She shook her head, her bright hair glinting deep russet in the lights. 'No. This is as far as I can go.'

Nadim dropped his hand, and his sense of foreboding increased just before Iseult hitched up her chin and said with quiet dignity, 'I'm afraid that I've done the exact thing you were so intent that I shouldn't do, Nadim: I've fallen in love with you.'

For a second her words didn't register. Everything was muffled, as if coming from far away, and Nadim actually had the very disturbing sensation for the first time in his life that he might faint. With a supreme act of will he stayed standing and felt anger rise. Anger at himself, for not trusting his instincts all along, and irrational anger at Iseult, for letting her emotions get involved. Anger that she was ruining this. And anger that she'd allowed him the power to hurt her. He'd learnt nothing.

'I don't believe you. You just want something from me. What is it? Commitment? An allowance? The promise of security for your family at home?'

She shook her head sadly. 'The only thing I want from you, Nadim, is the one thing I know you can't give me. Your love.'

An intense unnamed emotion rising up within him made Nadim lash out. He was barely aware of what he was saying any more—only aware that he had to push Iseult and her words back…far, far away. Everything he'd constructed around himself since Sara had died was being comprehensively threatened.

His voice was faintly scathing. 'What would you know about love?'

Iseult went very still before him, and immediately after he'd said the words he wished them unsaid. She paled in the dim light and turned away, her back looking too delicate. Nadim even reached out a hand, but dropped it when she turned back. Instead of the fire he'd expected, *wanted*, to see in her eyes, they looked dead now. And that was far worse.

Something within him was intensely moved by her innate dignity, compounded when she hitched her chin and looked him straight in the eye, unflinchingly. 'More than you, it would appear. I lost the two people I loved most in the world before I was thirteen and my world fell apart. I know about feeling so responsible for the people you love most that you can't sleep at night. I know about struggling so hard to make ends meet that it consumes you to the point where you forget you have choices in your life—but you don't care because you're doing it for someone you love.'

Nadim opened his mouth, but Iseult unwrapped her arms from her middle and cut him off with a slashing gesture of her hand. She moved a bit closer. Fire was returning to her eyes, faint colour to her cheeks. But Nadim didn't feel comforted. He felt as if he was watching something very precious break in front of his eyes.

The fierce look on her face forbade Nadim from speaking.

'I've fallen in love with you and I wish to God that I hadn't—believe me.' She smiled, but it was tight. 'Don't worry, you were perfectly clear all along the way, so I have no one to blame but myself. But I know it'll destroy me to continue to indulge in this dream world only to have it ripped away when you've had enough of this affair… I've lost too much already, Nadim. I can't wait passively by just to lose you too…'

The words died away into a heavy tense silence. Iseult felt numb. She couldn't believe she'd just said all she had, but his obvious horror at her declaration and the shameful surge of hope he'd dampened had sent a white-hot surge of anger through her: anger at herself for being so stupid. At no point had she intended this outpouring of her innermost feelings, and yet she knew now, facing him across this room, that she couldn't have contained it.

'That's why I want to go home, Nadim,' she said. 'To keep me here would be the worst form of cruelty, and I know you won't do that.'

She challenged him across the room with her

eyes. Nadim looked as if a lorry had just run into him. His face had leached of colour, his eyes were like two stark pools of black in his face.

In a harsh voice she'd never heard before he said, 'I don't want you to leave, Iseult. I want you to stay and be my mistress. I can't promise how long our liaison will last, but I can promise that you will be looked after—no matter what.' He continued, 'But if you insist that you cannot divorce your feelings from our physical relationship, then I will have to let you go.'

Iseult wasn't sure how she was still standing. She couldn't feel her legs any more, and her heart felt as if it was tearing in two. Somehow she managed to find her voice. 'Then I have to go.'

She turned to leave. As she put her hand on the door handle she heard from behind her, 'You won't even stay for Devil's Kiss?'

Iseult's torn heart clenched hard, and she closed her eyes for a moment. Her deluded brain could almost believe for a second that she'd heard something desperate in Nadim's voice, but it had to be her imagination. She couldn't bear to turn around and see the coldly arrogant look that would be on his face.

Realisation struck home hard: Nadim had somehow managed to eclipse even Devil's Kiss. And, no, she couldn't even stay for him.

Not able to say another word, Iseult just let her

silence speak her answer and left the room, closing the door softly behind her.

Nadim stood looking at the door, speechless and motionless for a long moment. In a blinding flash he realised that no matter what he'd just said Iseult had got to him on an emotional level he'd never experienced before. He turned around and, seeing something, went over to the small table where the photo of his wife sat in a frame. Her sweetly smiling face cut him straight to the quick and mocked him for the revelation—almost as if she was saying, *Now you know what it feels like.*

In a quick flash of anger so intense that it made his vision blur Nadim took the picture and threw it violently against a wall, where it shattered and fell to the ground.

CHAPTER FOURTEEN

Iseult's alarm went off and she stretched out a hand to turn it off, snuggling back under her warm duvet for another minute. The contrast between where she was now and where she'd been up until just a few days ago couldn't be more pronounced. It was winter in Ireland and it was dark outside—and freezing. With sickening inevitability she couldn't help her thoughts gravitating to the tall, dark, hard man who had turned her life around and upside down.

Missing Nadim was a physical ache—especially at night in bed. After their last conversation things had happened with scary swiftness; Nadim had obviously been eager to see the back of her and get on with his life. Jamilah had come to Iseult, and the two women had shared a look that spoke volumes. It had been Jamilah who had escorted Iseult to the plane in Al-Omar, driving her herself, after Iseult had said an emotional farewell to Devil's Kiss. Both women had been tearful saying goodbye, and Iseult had extracted a promise from Jamilah that she'd visit Ireland soon.

Iseult had left a note for Nadim in her room with a simple message:

Nadim, thank you for making me feel beautiful. It means more than you could ever know… With my love, always, Iseult.

Chagrin burned her now to think of it. Even then she hadn't been able to drum up the necessary self-defence to protect herself. She'd gushed again. She might as well have ripped her own heart out and handed it to him on a platter along with a knife and fork.

And then, guiltily, she'd seen the exquisite small golden bottle of perfume that Nadim had gifted her, and hadn't been able to leave it behind, so now she tortured herself every day with the scent that reminded her of him indelibly.

Resolutely she threw back the warm cover and sat up to put her feet on the cold wooden floor. It was over. The fairytale had come to an end. She'd been greeted at home by Mrs O'Brien's joyful tears, her father's bone-crushing hug, Murphy's slobbering tongue, and a farm and stud that had been comprehensively turned around in the short time she'd been gone. But they still needed her here. She was being kept busy from six a.m. until ten p.m., and that was the way she would get through this dark tunnel.

That evening, with darkness falling rapidly under a threatening sky, Iseult stood looking at the gallops, wrapped up against the cold in jeans and a polo neck and a thick parka jacket, with her favourite flat cap on her head. The last colt had just been returned to the stables for the evening by one of the new stablehands.

She was just realising that she was standing in exactly the same spot where Nadim had stood when she'd first laid eyes on him when she heard the low rumble of a powerful engine behind her.

Not expecting any visitors that evening, Iseult turned to see who it was—and her blood stopped in her veins when she saw a silver Jeep with tinted windows. And then the door opened and a familiar tall, dark figure got out. It was only the sound of the door shutting that made Iseult move jerkily away from the fence.

She thought she might be hallucinating, and spoke as much to convince herself that she wasn't as to acknowledge him. 'Nadim.'

He was dressed in dark jeans and a jumper, a worn black leather jacket. And he looked so exotic against the grey leaden skies that Iseult couldn't take another step in case she fell down.

For a wild and exhilarating second she thought

that he might have actually come for *her*—and then stomach-churning realisation hit her like a punch in the gut when she remembered how cold he'd been, how quickly he'd got her out of Merkazad. How he hadn't even said goodbye.

She walked forward and stumbled slightly, heart palpitating now with humiliation that for a second she'd thought— Ruthlessly she focused her wayward mind. 'You're here to see my father...or...or Peter the manager...? Well, Peter's gone home, but my father is up in the house. If you want to come up...'

Panic was rising through Iseult in waves—panic that he'd seen something of her helpless yearning reaction. He was standing there so implacably, looking so hard and stern, with dark stubble lining his jaw.

She'd never thought for a moment that she'd have to face him again so soon. This cruelty knew no bounds, and if she'd had the co-ordination she'd have marched over to him and hit him. Panic taking complete control now, Iseult whirled away and started to walk up the drive, not even feeling her legs move.

'Iseult, wait.'

Iseult stopped, breathing hard, but didn't turn around. She couldn't.

'I haven't come here to see your father or Peter. I've come to see you.'

Damn that exhilaration. It was snaking through her veins again. Still, resolutely, Iseult wouldn't turn around, terrified he'd see her reaction.

'I don't want to see you. I think you'd have to agree that we both know where we stand.' Her voice became bitter. 'I made my feelings quite clear.'

For a long moment there was silence. Iseult nearly started walking again, and then she heard from behind her, 'Ever since I laid eyes on you I've felt a pull stronger than anything I've ever felt before. My parents had an arranged marriage, and although they didn't love each other they had great affection and respect for one another. That's all I ever wanted and hoped for in a marriage, and no one ever came along to shake that assertion. Not even my wife. Sara was a good, kind, beautiful woman…but she knew she didn't have all of me. She went on the horse that day even though she was pregnant, even though she was terrified of them, because she wanted to impress me.'

Iseult was rooted to the spot, his words causing an ache in her chest. She was barely breathing.

'Sara died because she wanted me to fall in love with her. My respect and loyalty and affection weren't enough. Yet from the moment *we* met you reached right down inside me to a place Sara never could have touched. And the guilt of realising that has nearly killed me.'

Slowly, Iseult turned around to face Nadim. He stood there with an expression she'd never seen on his face. Vulnerability.

'What are you saying…?'

He grimaced. 'I'm saying that I almost let my guilt rule my life. I almost let my guilt convince me that I didn't love you… Every time I was telling you not to fall in love with me I was telling myself not to fall in love with you, because I thought I didn't deserve it. When we slept together I felt guilty, because Sara had never enjoyed making love. I felt guilty because you were so vibrant and brave and beautiful. I had no right to indulge in falling in love when I hadn't been able to fall in love with my own wife…and it had killed her and our baby.'

On a wave of immense love and compassion Iseult half walked and half ran to Nadim, raising shaking hands to his face. 'You weren't to blame for your feelings. If it was an arranged marriage there was every chance Sara wouldn't have loved you either… You never asked her to get on that horse. And she took her own life in her hands— and her unborn child's. Not you.'

Nadim raised a hand and put it over one of Iseult's, and pressed a kiss to her palm. His stubbled jaw tickled her skin, and she could see now that he looked tired, with lines around his mouth. His skin was slightly grey under his tan.

Hoarsely he said, 'I know that now. I think I've finally begun to forgive myself for Sara's death. The minute you walked into my life I think the healing started, and the minute you walked away from me I wanted you back. But I was stubborn, convinced you wouldn't have the guts to go. I thought you wouldn't be able to leave the luxury behind, no matter what you said.'

He quirked a wry smile. 'I should have known you better. Of course you went. And all I could manage was three days before going so crazy that I had to come after you. Guilt or no guilt.'

He pulled Iseult's cap off her head and sent it sailing in the wind, over the fence. 'Hey!' Iseult protested half-heartedly, her head spinning. 'I liked that cap.'

Nadim put his hands around Iseult's face and looked down into her eyes with such intensity that she felt as if she were drowning.

'Iseult, will you come back to Merkazad and marry me and be my wife?'

Her heart flip-flopped. Tears filled her eyes, but as much as she wanted to shout out *Yes!* she bit her lip. 'Don't you have to marry someone *suitable*?'

'*You* are the only suitable wife for me. I want you…no one else.'

Iseult clung onto the anchor of intensity in Nadim's eyes and face as he waited. Shakily she finally said, 'Then, yes...I'll marry you...even though I've no idea what that will make me.'

'What it will make you, *habiba*, is my beloved wife. You will be my Sheikha, by my side through thick and thin. Best friends. Lovers for ever.'

Iseult smiled tremulously. 'I like the sound of that... But you might have to coach me in some of the social situations—it's not my area of expertise. And I do have a chronic lack of self-esteem sometimes, but it's getting much better.'

A familiarly arrogant look crossed Nadim's face. 'You are beautiful, and I will tell you a thousand times a day until you believe it down to the depths of your being. And you will be with me in every situation. That's all you need to worry about.'

Finally, as if she'd been holding back, still protecting some vulnerable part of herself, Iseult pulled Nadim's head down to hers and pressed her mouth to his with a desperate fervour matched only by his own. He lifted her up and Iseult wrapped her legs around his waist. Her arms wound around his neck, and she knew that they would never let each other go again.

Six months later...

Iseult stood at the fence at al Saqr Stables, watching the new trainer with Devil's Kiss. He was getting closer and closer to being ready for the prestigious event at Longchamp later that year. Her pride in the horse was matched only by her pride in her beautiful husband, who arrived at that moment and snaked his arms around her waist, pulling her against him with possessive familiarity.

Iseult tipped back her head and Nadim pressed a kiss against her cheek. 'Where did you disappear off to this afternoon?'

Iseult savoured the moment, turning around in Nadim's arms so she could look up into his eyes. 'I had to go into town to see Dr Nadirah.'

Immediately Iseult felt tension come into Nadim's body. His arms tightened. 'Is there something wrong?'

She smiled and shook her head, and took his hand and placed it on her still-flat belly. And then she said, with a distinct wobble in her voice, 'Nothing. But about eight months from now we may well be suffering from periodic bouts of sleep-deprivation and a serious overload of love and joy…'

Nadim just looked down at her for a long, intense moment, and she saw everything in his expression. The poignant loss of his first baby, the residue of guilt, the fear of history repeating itself…

She put a hand to his jaw, caressing it. 'We deserve this, Nadim. *You* deserve this. And everything is going to be fine. I promise.'

He pulled her up against him and kissed her

so passionately that some approaching staff did a quick detour in the other direction. With Iseult's feet still dangling off the ground, Nadim finally stopped kissing her and threw back his head. He laughed out loud. A shout of pure joy.

And Iseult was right. Everything *was* fine.